D0686406

PLANET STORY

PLANET STORY

HARRY HARRISON JIM BURNS

A & W Visual Library—New York

First published in the United States of America in 1979 by
A & W Publishers, Inc.
95 Madison Avenue,
New York, New York 10016
By Arrangement with Pierrot Publishing Limited London.

Library of Congress Catalog Card Number—78-65675
ISBN 0-89104 135 4 (paperback)
0-89104 136 2 (hardcover)
Printed in Hong Kong.

CONTENTS

CHAPTER 1.

STR

EXILE TO ABISMUS

FASTER THAN A SPEEDING BULLET, faster than a beam of light, faster than anything in the galaxy, the space-battleship *U.S.E. Execrable* hurtled through the eternal night between the stars. Dark, ominous, as loomingly large as a small planetoid, marked with the gaping mouths of rocket tubes and blaster cannon, speckled with the bird shit of a thousand planets, it rushed through the blackness of interstellar space. Twelve thousand, two hundred and forty-three troopers called the old *Execrable* home, or would have called it home if they called their home a dismal, depressing, soul-destroying prison. Except for the sergeants and the officers, all were draftees, and all were miserable. And the most miserable of all was a trooper by the name of Parrts. He was the broken and bottom-most rung on the tallest ladder, the

hangnail on the fractured toe of the last leper, the lowermost dingleberry on the rump of the oldest cow on the most backward planet. He was in trouble.

"Private Parrts you are in trouble," the Over-Sergeant growled feelingly. The Sergeant was short, pot-bellied, wrinkled as a toad, with skin the colour of a mummified crocodile and a growth of beard like a wire brush. "You do find me attractive, Parrts, don't you? Just a little-wittle bit?" He grabbed Parrts by the left buttock, leaving claw marks.

"No Sergeant, I think you're kind of ugly."

"And that's just what you told Doctor-Psychiatrist Wankle," roared the Sergeant. "So what if her tits rattle on her kneecaps when she walks, so what if her face looks like a buffalo's bum – you got no right to talk to an officer that way!"

"She had no right to pull me off guard duty, wearing a purple nightgown, and into her quarters and..."

"What were you doing wearing a purple nightgown on guard duty?"

"Don't attempt to obfuscate the issue, Sergeant, I was doing my duty and she had no right..."

"Shut up and listen, Private. You got no rights. You are a trooper. An officer says 'dog' and you bark. You are in big trouble and the only way you are going to get out of it is by giving me a big kiss and slipping into my sack. Yes?"

"No."

The Sergeant sighed, deeply and movingly and his breath was like a strong wind from the garbage dump. A tear, looking very much like a drop of nitro-glycerine, formed in the corner of his eye. "Then you are really up the creek," he said. "You have been sowing dissension and despair among this crew–"

"But they have been making passes at me! You just did it yourself..."

"Shut up," the Sergeant hinted. "If we were at war you would be garrotted or shot, but it will be at least a week before the war starts again. So the captain has done the next best thing and you will be assigned to the Resupply Base on Strabismus when we stop there."

"What's so bad about that?"

"I'm glad you asked. Strabismus is a chill, worthless, rotten planet which is halfway from nowhere to nowhere. But if you look at it from a different angle it is halfway from somewhere to somewhere, namely between Good Old Mother Earth, may she rule for ever, and the decadent planets of the Outer Marches where we are teaching the aliens a thing or two about civilization. Therefore we have the Resupply Base on Strabismus to care for our weary spacefarers, to supply food and drink to the hungry and thirsty, to provide spare parts for those whose spares have parted. The Resupply Base is fully automated and can service the hulkingest battleship, the teeniest scout ship, in a matter of moments, at a touch of a button. It needs no attention or maintenance, service or supervision. That is why you are being assigned there."

"You mean I'll be alone!" Parrts was ecstatic with joy.

"Not in this man's army, Private Parrts. We exist to make you miserable, not happy. There is a commander of the Resupply Base, who feels he should have more than robots to command. He wants troops. You, Trooper, will be his troops."

"I don't understand..."

"You will when I tell you his name. He is...Colonel Kylling."

Parrts's cry of pain rang out like that of a tormented soul in hell.

"I thought you might like that," the Sergeant smiled with evil relish. He looked at the watch set into his navel. "You have just enough time to write your last will, go to confession, or commit suicide before we land."

"Well screw *you*, Sergeant!"

"Yes, please!" the Sergeant said with a glad cry, leaping forward, only to be rebuffed by the slam of the bulkhead door. He emitted a shuddering sigh and flicked the pendant tear from his eye . . . which exploded when it hit the deck.

"No justice," Private Parrts seethed to himself as he stamped down the corridor, *"no justice at all."* Not that he expected justice, quite the contrary, but it would just be nice to see a little for a change. Or would it? The only thing the military service was consistent in was its injustice and he realized that he had come to rely on it. A benchmark in the wilderness of existence. Something to supply the needed reassurance that no matter how bad it was it was sure to get worse. And maybe someday he would get home and find his local draft board and shoot every member of it.

His current problem had started there. By inclination he was an historian; by shrewd decision an exobiologist. Early on in his historical studies he had seen the handwriting clearly on his tombstone. Get into a reserved occupation or get killed in the Troopers. It did not take an historian to identify the pseudo-feudal, superficially-imperial, obviously military-fascistic United States of Earth as a bad deal for anyone on the bottom of the pile. When a government is fighting a galactic war on an ever-expanding spherical front line it also does not take a mathematical genius to see that enemies – and all aliens were of course enemies because they were alien – would continue to be discovered at a rate equal to the cube squared. Even the most ambitious military building plan and the most exacting draft standards would have instantly to fall behind the needs of the front line commanders. They grew hoarse shouting for equipment and troops. Draft boards who did not produce found themselves in boot camp themselves to fill their quotas. At the time when Parrts had decided that a career as an historian was not for him the minimum draft age had been nine. He had been eight when he made this important decision. His father had been drafted just seven seconds after Parrts had been conceived; his mother's bio-telltale had lit up with a red "pregnant" light the instant his father's sperm had plunged headlong into her waiting ovum. Despite the fact that his father had sired twelve children for the good of the U.S. of E., had a double hernia, a missing left leg and a glass right eye, he was still draft fodder. Standards had changed since he had been invalided out of the Troopers a few years earlier. During the seven months that it took Parrts to get born (accelerated parturition helped the draft too) the standards changed once again and his mother went straight from the delivery room to boot camp, for sex was no longer a barrier to the call of the draft. Nor was age; the Sergeant Nurses-aide who took care of her was her own grandmother.

Parrts grew up in a Home for Future Troopers so was not completely unaware of the whither of the world. Despite all the careful propaganda, the inmates of the home developed a shrewd idea about the nature of war; easy enough when all of one's teachers are quadruple amputees. So Parrts understood that, while he could carry on his historical pursuits as a hobby, his life's vocation had better be something that would keep him out of the cannon-fodder category. Since he was first in his class he opted for exobiology; the study of alien life. This was interesting enough in its own right, but more important it carried the very highest military disqualification number in the book, which was the real reason he picked it. The military needed biological knowledge of the enemy, in order to find new ways of killing them, so Parrts knew he would be in a reserved and protected profession.

So much for plans. Everything worked fine for a number of years until, during one of his monthly checks with his draft board to have his deferment stamped. The former chairman of the draft board had been drafted, the closer the flame the

hotter the burn, and the new chairperson was named Annabella O'Brien. Ex-commando Sergeant O'Brien, if the whole truth be known. As soon as Parrts walked through the door she smiled a thin smile, on lips that had seen no smile for years, dismissed the rest of the draft board, locked the door and got Parrts in a Maltese hammerhold. This involved locking one arm around his neck and almost smothering him in the vale between her massive breasts, while with her free hand she frantically dialled the combination on the lock of his magnetic flies. Parrts could only struggle in vain against his mighty opponent's unbreakable grip, until his flapping hand found the desk set from which, in the last throes of suffocation, he extracted the pen and jabbed it into her arse. She had flung her arms wide, with good reason, and he had crawled beneath the long desk and kicked feebly at her groping hand while he fought oxygen back into his starving cells. After two hours she had, dimly, received the message that he wasn't her type and in a fit of girlish pique had classified him 1A. Parrts was out of the door within seconds and in boot camp hours before she had a good cry and a good drunk and had busted up four bars in the worst part of town.

It was the story of his life. Things went from worse to worse. And now this assignment on Strabismus with Colonel Kylling. His body temperature went down ten degrees as he thought about the man's reputation. But facts were needed, something better than latrine rumour. With his carefully stored jellybean ration Parrts bribed the record clerk to get a transcript of Kylling's military record. It made sordid reading indeed and Parrts became more and more depressed as he read faster and faster. For the paper was growing red in his fingers, then brown, hotter and hotter before it burst into flame. He wouldn't be able to use it to blackmail the record clerk after all. But literally burned in words of fire, the record hung before his eyes. Colonel Kylling was...

"Action stations. Prepare for landing." The subsonic sirens blasted through every compartment of the ship and softened the bones in the bodies of those who did not move fast enough. Parrts moved. He stood at the main power switch in the engine room, rigidly at attention, doing the job he had been so painstakingly trained for. He stood there, immobile, as the incredible bulk of the *Execrable* dropped down through the planetary atmosphere of Strabismus. Through the thick layers of cloud and into the clear air again, stern jets roaring, to set down light as a falling feather on the landing pad. "SET DOWN" the illuminated panel read and Parrts instantly pressed the "OFF" button. He sighed, his job completed, perhaps for the last time. Surely the last time, for the records had been clear on one thing. Men entered Colonel Kylling's outfit; none had ever been known to leave. Alive.

"Private Parrts," the wall speaker roared. "Get your gear and get to the main port on the double."

He did as ordered, his bag on his shoulder, walking alone through the twenty metre high portal, dodging the rushing robots with their supplies and ammunition. There was a drink dispensing machine in the crew room beyond and he dropped his bag and put in some coins and pushed the controls for a heroin-cola, then mixed it with a hash-soda. He had no future, it did not matter. Although he knew he was alone, had to be alone, he nevertheless felt eyes upon him. He twitched and turned – and the cup fell from his suddenly nerveless fingers.

Colonel Kylling was staring at him. No, that word isn't adequate, does not express the horror of the man's gaze. Rather he impaled Parrts with the glare of his single eye. The other eye had been gouged out, or eaten out or something equally nasty, leaving a singularly repulsive scarred pit uncovered by a patch or glass eye. Kylling stood as immobile as a lizard, looking very much like one in fact with his bald, scarred skull tightly covered in greenish skin.

The eye glared, the gaping nostrils flared furrily, for the hair missing from the head had apparently sunk into these shaggy caverns. Both of the protruding ears obviously had pieces bitten out of them. The crushed convolutions of the nose are best left undescribed. The man's jaw, however, would have made a Neanderthal jealous. It was as prognathous as the bucket of a power-shovel, sticking out so far forward that all the yellowed and jagged tombstone teeth projected up over his upper lip, a few actually nestling neatly in the furry comfort of his nose.

"Well," the Colonel growled, in a slimy sort of gravelly voice, "what do you think you are looking at?"

The impossibility of answering this question, for in addition to the face there were the anthropoid arms, knuckles resting on the deck, pot-belly and bowed legs, froze Parrts into paralysed silence. He stiffened to attention while the glare of the single eye swept up and down him like a laser-powered paralysis beam that left scorch marks on his uniform. Then Kylling shuffled forward slamming his riding crop into his palm as he came. Parrts felt the blood congeal in his veins when he realized that the crop was not leather but was the mummified and shrunken body of a trooper, the corporal's stripes still visible on the mummified and shrunken uniform. Kylling shambled in a circle about Parrts, muttering savagely to himself. Parrts drew in a shuddering gasping breath.

"Did I give you permission to breathe?" Kylling said in a voice so drenched with menace that Parrts's lungs instantly froze. The silent inspection went on and the blackness of asphyxiation and sure death fell over Parrts. At the last moment, really a few moments past the last moment – Parrts' IQ dropped six points as his brain cells were knocked off – Kylling snapped the order. "Resume breathing."

The veil of darkness lifted, life-giving air rushed in, and Parrts could no longer remember the seven times table.

"What are you doing here?" the Colonel rumbled.

"Assigned to this base, sir. Orders in my bag."

"I requested a company of non-returnable, death-sentenced prisoners. And all I get is you."

"I'll get back in the ship, sir, if you like..."

"DON'T MOVE!"

Kylling's roar was so loud that it almost drowned out the roar of the spaceship taking off. Parrts's last hope was gone. He relaxed and faced the end.

"I'll get my company of expendables yet. Meanwhile you will have to do. What have you heard about me, Private?"

"Nothing good, sir."

"Well the message is getting out, albeit dimly. Details, Private, what interesting things do the troopers say about me when they loll around wanking in the evenings?"

"They say, sir, that you are the most free-wheeling, treacherous, murderous son of a bitch since armies were invented. Attila would have been your second in command. You have never lost a battle or brought a trooper back alive. Your personal life is a warped mélange of bigotry, sadism, masochism, torture, flagellation and mass murder."

"So word *is* getting around! How very nice." Kylling smiled and nodded with pleasure, thwacking the shrunken skull of the corporal against the steel toe of his boot. "Anything else? Be frank."

"Why, yes sir. Your record says that..." Parrts's voice drained away and his jaw dropped as he gaped at the Colonel. "Why there is nothing in the record about... no, nothing... not a word about sex at all." Parrts broke into a broad grin and stuck out his right hand. "Put her there, Colonel, it'll be a pleasure to serve with you."

Colonel Kylling roared like a herniated lion in heat and leapt forward, fingers arched and yellowed claws ready, his breath foul as an elephants' graveyard in summer.

THE QU
LIF

CHAPTER 2.

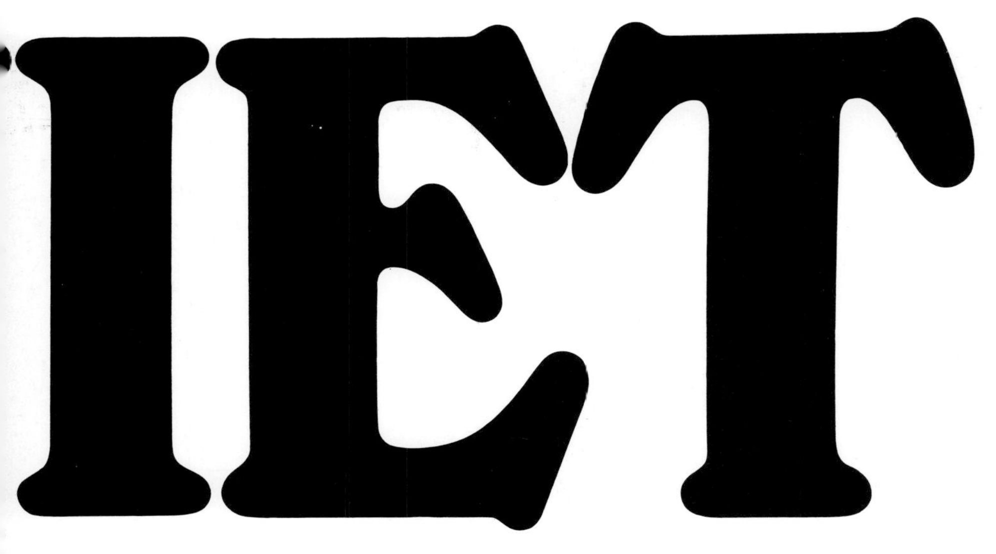

"NO!" PARRTS CRIED, falling back, raising his hands in feeble defence. "You misunderstand. I *like* you, sir. It is a pleasure to serve under you. I can explain."

Colonel Kylling hesitated, astonished, confused. No one liked him; that was the order of things. He thought, for long ticking seconds, then grunted. And reached into a pocket, removed a minigrenade, twisted the actuator, then tucked it into the top of Parrts's boot.

"You have one minute to explain. If the explanation is not satisfactory that grenade will blow your legs off. Then, using my fingernails alone, I will claw your stomach open, whip out your intestines and strangle you with them..."

"All right, Colonel, I know you know all about that sort of thing. You're on my time now." Parrts talked swiftly, faster and faster, sweat breaking out on his forehead. "You see, sir, I have led a very interesting life – not as interesting as yours of course. It seems that I have what might be called a rather unusual power, or psionic radiation or some such. I would make a very interesting subject for study by a university, of course if the war wasn't on, because I radiate what I must call, for lack of a better term, an overpowering sexuality. Or sex appeal. No, sir, I beg of you, don't grate your teeth like that or you will cut your nose. So, fine you might say, but only at first sight. Or perhaps if only nubile young girls found me attractive I might find myself being washed through life on a sea of requited love, but it is not that simple. *Everyone* loves me, every *thing* in fact. I cannot walk down the street without every stray dog embracing my leg – you should see the state of my trousers at times! But that is another story, right, I hear the tick-tick! Talk fast. I cannot ride a horse because the horse has only one thing on its mind. I would be dead in ten seconds on a dairy farm. The ugliest old man, the sweetest young child, yearn only for one thing from me. Life is hell, I tell you. You might laugh ha-ha, but you put up with it for twenty years. It's like working in a chocolate factory and not wanting to eat sweets. Do you want to kiss me, sir?"

Kylling roared in anger, mouth gaping so wide that not only were his tonsils visible but the remains of his last meal in his stomach as well.

"There, see now what I mean, sir? You are the only man, woman, beast, creature, insect that does not find me lovable. It is a pleasure to be in your command, sir. I am at your orders. Shall I whip you – or do you want to whip me?"

The Colonel thought and thought and there was a warm sizzling sound from the top of Parrts's boot. Then one long and grimy fingernail flashed out, the grenade went flying to explode against the vending machine with a mini roar. Noxious beverages leaked out and bubbled darkly on the floor.

"I'm not sure I like it," the Colonel muttered.

"Volunteers don't really work in this sort of job. Oh a good masochist is jolly fun, laughing away as the flesh peels from the bones. You aren't a crypto-masochist, are you?"

"No, sir, but I would be willing to try..."

"No damn good!"

"Well I would make a good batman, sir." Parrts

on 1
freeze
oro
enhance
i·red
x·ray
zoom
store
q·slant

on 2
freeze
oro
enhance
i·red
x·ray
zoom
store
q/slant

smiled his most fetching smile. "Clean the blood from your boots. Sharpen the steel spikes on their soles. Keep the lead molten, the barbed wire rusty. . ."

"Arrrghh!" the Colonel snarled as he stamped heavily away. Parrts grinned, as happy as he had ever been in his lifetime, shouldered his bag and whistled and whistled while he looked for the EM's quarters.

So began the happiest days of his life. There was little or no work to do since the base was completely automated. He cracked into the library stores and resumed with pleasure his historical studies. When his eyes grew tired he would leave the base for some fresh air. The base was of course not meant to be left but it was easy enough work to disconnect the internal alarms and drill through the ferroconcrete outer wall with a combat laser. The weather outside was uniformly chill, but refreshing. A mountaintop had been sheered off and levelled and the base built upon it. Other snowclad mountains stood about and clouds rolled damply up from the unseen valleys below. No signs of native life forms were visible. It would often snow and Parrts would make a snowman with bullets for eyes and a grenade for a nose then, red-cheeked and happy, would return to his books.

He rarely saw the Colonel who brooded alone in his quarters, thinking up violent and revolting scenes. Occasionally he would seek Parrts out and threaten him with them, but the Trooper's willingness to help took away all the fun. Colonel Kylling took to drinking heavily in his private torture chamber, fondling the instruments and smiling at the memories the stains of dried blood brought forth.

But at the door of every Eden there is a serpent waiting to enter. Spaceships, large and small, came and went, but Parrts hid while they were on the ground. Once he even admired the image of the luscious pilot of a scoutship and thought that one day he might seek solace in arms as lovely as hers. But not right away.

The serpent knocked on the gate. A transport slid in close above the atmosphere and dropped a landing capsule. This cracked open to disgorge a single occupant and a great deal of heavy equipment. The man, a thin and seedy-looking individual with a wispy grey beard and terminal acne, checked his crates then plugged into the viewscreen.

"Professor Shlek here, calling the commanding officer. Come in at once."

Colonel Kylling, who was happily at work with some broken glass modifying his rack, looked at the viewscreen with disgust, then rang for his assistant.

"Waiting to be commanded, sir," was the instant response.

"Private Parrts, get out on the pad and see what that dismal-looking turkey wants. Check his priority at once. If it's thirteen or lower get him into the dungeon and there'll be a hot time in the old town tonight. They'll never bother to check on a low priority. Move!"

Parrts flipped aside the *History of Royal Alliances and Treacherous Affiliations from the Thirteenth to the Twenty-second Century* and exited. Prof. Shlek glared at him, then swallowed heavily and his eyes widened as the Trooper grew close. Parrts recognized the symptoms and kept his distance. "How can we help you, sir," he asked. "And could I see your papers please. Commander's orders."

Parrts flipped through the document. Three-B. Too bad. The Colonel would be miffed. But the priority was too high to take chances. While he read he kept a careful eye on Shlek who was rummaging through his boxes, vanishing from sight behind the pile. He grabbed the opportunity to whisper into his collar microphone a quick report to the Colonel, getting only an acid grumble in return and a sharp disconnect.

"I have a very important assignment," Prof. Shlek said, still hid by the mountain of crates. "I have been ordered by the Planetary Survey Corps to do a planetary survey of Strabismus. Only a rough prelim

41
PRIORITY
3B

was done before this base was made. Now they want the complete job and it has to be done in a single day because that is when the next ship is picking me up, so I have to rush and you had better help me or else. I gotta lot of clout, Trooper. Cross me and you are in it up to your neck. Help me and I can do you a favour or two. Now we are in a big rush, but not *that* big a rush..."

Shlek appeared, swaying and simpering in high heels. He had slipped into a very sexy black dress, low cut over his falsies, and wore a bright red wig. He had bungled the lipstick though, smearing it in his passionate hurry.

"We must be quick, but there is more than enough time for a big kiss, you passionate brute you, and even better..."

What was even better was the smart *chok* of Parrts's fist getting the Professor on his glass jaw and decking him.

"Brute," Shlek cried, then hissed "You'll pay for that."

"No I won't because this encounter has been surveilled and taped and will be cut right after you hit the ground and the word will go out that my accidental punch killed you. But that won't be what killed you for you will have experienced twenty-four hours at the hands of Colonel Kylling, commander of this base..."

Shlek screamed shrilly and began tearing off the dress, stripping right down to his sequined jockstrap, then hurrying into his uniform, sniffling his ready tears as he went. It was all a boring rerun to Parrts who had been here far too often before. When Shlek had pulled himself together and restocked his wardrobe the survey began.

It was obvious after very few minutes that Prof. Shlek really needed no help at all in setting up his equipment. The request for aid had only been an excuse to make a pass at whoever appeared. No more was said about the incident – but Parrts kept his eyes peeled and his fist ready. Shlek, involved in his work, ignored him.

The largest crate of all dropped open to reveal a survey satellite already in its launching rack. Shlek muttered over his figures for planetary density and atmospheric gradients and set the controls accordingly. Given these parameters the robot brain in the rocket would automatically carry out the survey as specified. Shlek slammed shut the access port and locked it, then carried his control box a good hundred metres from the rocket. Parrts tailed after him, interested in the operation.

"If you're nice to me I'll let you press the button to start it off. It's great fun..."

Shlek's voice trailed away at the deep rattle of Parrts's growl. Miffed, he pressed the button himself. The rocket responded satisfactorily, and with a great rumble, roar and cloud of smoke it blasted into the sky and out of sight. Shlek looked at the control readout and nodded happily.

"All automatic, wonderful," he enthused. "Not like the old days when you had to program the things every metre of the way. It's off now on a spiral orbit meshed in with the planet's rotation, nipping along just outside the atmosphere. Working hard. Continuous infra-red and ultra-violet recording, magnetometer and Xibla wave analysis that can spot any minerals up to three kilometres under the surface. Surface temperature readings, water vapour and...YEOW! You've broken my wrist! I barely touched you..."

"You want some chow. I'll bring it to you out here. Or should I send the Colonel...?"

"Food! Lovely troopers' rations. Reconstituted desiccated dog meat stew. Nutritious wood-pulp bread. Yum!"

Thoughts of the Colonel's hobbies had caused Shlek to slip a cog. Parrts nodded agreement. He had long since broken into the staff officers' ration store and was thinking more of pheasant under glass and roast boar's head. But if Shlek wanted troopers' chow that's what he was getting.

It was hours after dark before the survey rocket finished its task. Shlek was bright blue and shivering with cold. Parrts almost felt sorry for him. Almost. The surveyor zeroed in on their radio beacon, fired its retro-rockets – a red light among the stars – then cracked its parachute and touched the ground mere seconds after it had opened. It lay on its side, steaming and crackling, and Shlek gingerly opened the panel and removed the rolls of tape.

"In-n-side," he chattered. "L-load this thing in the morning."

Parrts carried the analyser and followed after the tottering Professor. In the warmth of the transient quarters, with a pint of hot cawfee-eck inside him, Shlek thawed out enough to feed the tape into the machine. It hummed happily, needles flickered and numbers flashed.

"Usual junk," Shlek muttered. "Iron, we get all we need from the asteroid belts. Gold, waste product of the desalination plants. Sulphur, copper, uranium – too small a deposit that one – lead, Lortium . . . *Lortium!*" He jumped to the controls, pushing buttons madly, then grabbed the printout as it emerged from its slot. "It's there! What a find, rich, big, yum! I'll get a finder's bonus and get laid at last. Whee!"

"What's Lortium?" Parrts asked.

"A bullying, low I. Q. trooper like you would have no idea. It's a transplutonic element, the rarest. It's needed for the powerplants in the big battleships. It makes war possible."

"Tell them you didn't find it. Maybe the war will stop."

"Are you out of your weensy mind? Without a war I'd be out of a job and a gunsil in a drag cathouse. Besides, there's a duplicate tape sealed in the rocket. They trust me as much as they trust you."

"Zero."

"That's right. Now get out so I can get drunk and cry myself to sleep with my dolly. Got to be up at dawn to scout the site."

Parrts was there as well in the chill fog of daybreak. He had an uneasy feeling that this discovery was going to change his idyllic existence. He looked at Shlek's thin neck and thought maybe he ought to turn him over to the Colonel and have the robots push all the survey equipment off the edge of the cliff. No, wouldn't work. Shlek's priority would cause an investigation and another survey man would be sent. He watched glumly as the sampler rocket blasted away. It would circle the site, photograph it, then drill its way down through the surface to get a sample of the ore. In less than two hours it came whistling back and plopped down beside them. Shlek drew out the sample with quivering fingers, poked it, tasted a bit and nodded happily.

"Rich, really rich!"he cackled. "I've got it made! You, boy, get the robots to reload my equipment so I'll be ready for the ship." He was so excited that he didn't even make a pass, which was the only good part of an otherwise depressing day.

Slow as the military were at issuing pay, rations and pro-kits, they were efficiency itself when it came to digging up Lortium. Commands, instructions and queries crackled through the ether and Parrts spent long hours in the communications room. Colonel Kylling watched all this activity with growing excitement. "Lortium can be dangerous stuff," he said. "Radioactive, poisonous. They'll need hardened criminals to dig it . . .

"And maybe we can purloin a prisoner or two."

The Colonel made a strange wheezing sound that Parrts had learned to recognize as sadistic laughter. "I'm going to oil the rack and sharpen the spikes in the iron maiden," he said, and exited.

The final communication simply read "RRAGG ARRIVING TWENTY HOURS".

"Who – or what – is RRAGG?" Parrts asked and, since he was alone in the room, he naturally received no answer.

CHAPTER 3.

ENTER RRAGG

"THAT'S THE LARGEST spacebarge I have ever seen, Colonel."

"Shut up or I'll thrash you until you scream."

"Sure, Colonel. Which whip do you want?"

"Arrrh," the colonel growled and slapped himself on the stomach and screamed "Arrrh!" again, only

REALTIME
MINUS 20
IDENT
INCOM

REALTIME MINUS SECS 43·3
TRAKERROR ZERO
ALTERROR ZERO
NT .... IDENT IDENT .... IDENT
..... EARTH » STRABISMUS FOXTROT SIX SIX ZERO TWO
TYPE 16 GIGABARGE
FLEET SERIAL SB(S)441 U.S.E.
(NON-HOSTILE)
REALTIME STATUS FINALS
L PAD WEIGHT STRAIN SENSOR
PREDICTION OVERLOAD!!!

louder. He had taken to wearing barbed wire under his shirt and hitting it when he felt depressed. He had to torture *somebody.*

The spacebarge was a gleaming cylinder of metal that looked as big as a battleship. Eight rocket tugs were locked onto it with full sternjets flaring, fighting the gravity of Strabismus that pulled at the giant object. Slower and slower the thing dropped until it settled to the ground, neatly crushing one corner of the Resupply Depot. Magnetic grapples were released and seven of the tugs instantly shot skywards and vanished. The eighth dropped to the pad and its entrance hatch ground open. A man emerged and Colonel Kylling stared at him with burning eye; visions of thumbscrews danced in his head.

"Are you RRAGG?" the Colonel asked.

"I am not," the man said, stopping a good three paces away, holding his case tightly to him, eyeing both of them suspiciously. "I am Captain Frig. RRAGG is in there."

"Come inside and have a drink," the Colonel cooed, "and tell me about it."

"Are you out of your teeny-tiny? I know your reputation, Colonel." Frig whipped some papers from the case. "I'll need your signature here, here, and here as receipt for RRAGG."

"You'll see nothing until *I* see what the hell it is that you have dropped on top of my station."

"If you insist," Frig sniffed. As he started forward he saw Parrts for the first time and his eyes widened and his nostrils flared. "Why hello there..."

"Keep moving, slob," Parrts grated, "or you'll be talking with a squeaky voice for the rest of your life."

Rebuffed and rejected, desiring and undesired, the newcomer walked swiftly to the side of the looming wall of metal and threw open a panel. He pressed a button inside and the massive end fell off and clanged to the ground.

"RRAGG, come out boy," he called, then whistled shrilly.

There was an echoing rumbling roar from the dark interior of the massive spacebarge followed by an ear-smashing metallic crashing. The roar grew louder and louder, and from the interior hurtled RRAGG. Crashing out until the solid rock crumbled, skidding to a stop in a storm of gravel and a cloud of dust, stopping, immobile yet waiting for orders, panting like a locomotive-sized hound dog.

"What the hell is that thing?" the Colonel said, unimpressed, looking up at the treads, wheels, pivoted arms, gears, buckets, drills, lights, pistons, pumps, lasers, and such junk.

"RRAGG is the acronym for Railroad and Ground Grader. This son of a bitch is the greatest railroad builder in the galaxy and a joy to see in action." A sonic pickup and eye swivelled towards him as he talked and the panting sound increased with his words. Far above a steam whistle screamed shrilly. Frig kicked a giant tread affectionately. "Completely self-controlled. RRAGG is no mere robot, but a high-powered brain that probably has an IQ bigger than both you dummies put together." The whistle sounded again and the Colonel lurched forward growling, his shrunken-corporal swagger stick raised for a killing blow. A blast of compressed air issued from RRAGG catching the Colonel and spinning him about, knocking him to the ground. "RRAGG knows who his friends are," Frig smirked.

He extended the papers to the fallen Colonel who placed them on the ground and, cursing, signed them. "Now that's more like it," Frig said. "One question before I depart. Here is a survey picture taken of the proposed mine site. I see it is located close to the north pole of this miserable planet, permanently covered in snow and ice and looking about as attractive as you, Colonel. And this dump here looks no better. Now RRAGG is ready to go at a moment's notice. He will build a railroad directly to the specified site and has been programmed with its location. When the railroad is done he will signal the

tugs who will drop down with the spacebarge and pick him up. Do you stupes follow this so far?"

The Colonel was on his feet in an instant and lurching forward, Parrts just behind him. Before they had taken two steps an artificial lightning bolt blasted into the stone before them blowing a deep pit. They lurched back. Smiling, the obnoxious newcomer held up a cigar and another lightning bolt lit it for him.

"Good boys – you do learn fast. Okay, so RRAGG knows where he is going, he knows where he is now. Before he starts I got one question to ask and maybe you pinheads can answer it. That moron planetary surveyor who did this job never looked at the surface of this planet so I don't know if it is inhabited or not. Other than with the pair of you, which is no bargain. If there are natives RRAGG goes around them for reasons that should be obvious even to you two. If it's jungle, ice, snow, snakes, the usual crap he just blasts on through. So which is it?"

"Uninhabited," the Colonel said. "Now get the hell off my planet."

"I saw a bird once," Parrts said. "But no one has ever been off this mountain so we don't really know. I think..."

"Shut up," the Colonel suggested. "And move this animated junk pile and move yourself before I lose my temper."

"Delighted, I assure you." Captain Frig packed away his papers, walked over to RRAGG and gave him a pat on the riveted hide, then reached up to a large red handle. It pointed straight down. On the left was stencilled "UNINHABITED," on the right "INHABITED." Seizing it in both hands he pulled and it slowly moved to the left. When it did a number of lights flashed on and off above and a laser beam shot a hole in the low-hanging clouds. The panting sound increased and the treads trembled. Frig stepped back, took his case from under his arm and extracted a bone from it. Then, with all his might, he threw it towards the edge of the plateau.

"Go get it, boy!" he shouted.

Whistles shrieked, engines roared, gears spun and the entire gigantic machine lurched forward, faster and faster, heading straight at the edge of the plateau, to the straight drop to the ground, kilometers below.

"Make a fine noise when it hits the bottom." The Colonel smiled.

But RRAGG was already at work. From the front a steel framework was being extruded, assembled by flashing arms even as it emerged. RRAGG barely hesitated on the brink as it extended the bridge structure across to the next mountain top. Laser beams seared ahead of it, carving buttresses and supports from the solid rock, ready to receive the far end when it arrived. No sooner had it settled into place than the great machine was roaring at speed across the span. And whenever it moved, fresh-laid railroad track emerged from its rear, across the plateau and across the bridge and away. Then, just before it reached the other mountain and the solid rock, its laser beams ravened forth again making an instant tunnel. It plunged headlong into this tunnel and, an instant before its sleeper-and-rail defecating rear vanished from sight, a laser blinked one last time. Parrts and the Colonel threw themselves aside as it blackened and seared the rock close by. Then RRAGG vanished from sight, silence descended and they saw the black letters burned into the solid stone.

RRAGG RULES, O.K.! it read.

The Colonel spun on his heel with a cry of rage – but he was too late. His prey, with his protector removed, had whisked himself to the spacetug and the port was just closing. The blast from the gun the Colonel had built into the shrunken corporal's head seared harmlessly on the metal.

Parrts sighed with relief. It had worked out far better than he had hoped, for the time being. He went back to his books. Hammering at his barbed wire truss the Colonel went back and played some of his own home movies to cheer himself up.

Neither would have been quite as happy if they had been following RRAGG's journey across the surface of Strabismus. Intelligent the great machine may have been; smart it was not. It could build a railroad better than any person or thing in the galaxy. A three-year-old human with a runny nose had more sense than it ever would have.

Happy at its work, RRAGG roared on. Down the high mountain range, drilling tunnels and spanning gulfs with ease, laying the finest railroad possible. Lower and lower, past the tree-level and below the eternal snows. Across one last valley, filled with a raging torrent, and into the cliff beyond. Downward, ever downward at an easy one in twelve grade. Sensing the end of the rock ahead and slowing and stopping as its front end emerged. A valley, warmer, plenty of vegetation, no problem just burn it out of the way; a river to span, better allow for an extra wide bridge for seasonal floods. No difficulties here. One victorious blast on the whistle and RRAGG lurched forward again. Across the valley and into the low hill beyond. Simple.

"Simple?" This giant machine was simple. Since the red handle was set at "UNINHABITED" its circuit could not see what any other living creature could have seen.

There was a small city by the water's edge. Peaceful orange aliens plied the water in delicate boats, sat on the poles before their homes playing musical instruments shaped like urinals, chanted mournful tunes on the stone steps of their temple.

Into this Elysian scene plunged RRAGG.

Into the city, through the city, laying track across the crushed remains of the homes. cutting half the temple away, planting bridge piers on top of the boats. A demon of destruction that came and went in an instant, its wailing whistle echoing the wails of the stunned and maimed survivors.

Something new had come to Strabismus.

INHABITED

CHAPTER 4.

S

& THE

TYREEN
BIG BOY

"IT'S ADMIRAL SODDY AGAIN, Colonel. He insists on talking to you personally," Parrts said.

"Tell him to . . ."

"I wouldn't live very long if I did, sir."

Kylling whipped the etherphone handpiece away from Parrts and oozed charm into the mouthpiece.

"Yes, Admiral, always a pleasure to talk to you. No, no location reports from RRAGG since the last one. It reports once an hour, very prompt about it, twenty-four hours a day. We don't get much sleep... yes, sir, I'm sure you feel sorry for me, no matter how you express the concern. Yes sir, we'll call as soon as the report comes in. You foul-smelling bastard offspring of a Mongolian goat and a gorilla."

Parrts looks up, startled, then relaxed when he saw that the Colonel had switched the etherphone off. Kylling rattled the handpiece against his teeth and mused. "I wonder why Soddy has such a big interest in the Lortium deposit? More powerplants for more ships?"

"No, sir, he doesn't care about the Lortium."

"No games, Private Parrts, no riddles. Not today."

"Perhaps you shouldn't sleep in your thumbtack girdle . . ."

"Save the advice. What's this about the Admiral?"

"I hear that he is a railroad nut. He is the one who had RRAGG built, who ordered the railroad built here against the advice of his technical officer who is now in the brig . . ."

"Send him here!"

"I have been trying to arrange it, sir. Sort of surprise for you. Anyway it would have been a lot easier to build a refinery and smelter complex someplace else on this planet rather than in these mountains, plus a pad for the ships to come and get the Lortium. The Admiral wouldn't hear of it. He wants a railroad so he gets . . ."

"This is RRAGG. Do you read me?" The mechanical voice crackled from the speaker. Parrts turned down the volume and picked up the mike.

"Ready for your report, RRAGG."

"Thirteen kilometres of track laid since last report. I am under the icecap now so am tunnelling through bedrock. Therefore advancing rate slowed."

"Will you give us a revised ETA at the mine site?"

"Don't know. Rock could change. Too many random factors. Estimate refused."

"Listen, you tracklaying junkyard, I couldn't care less if you got to the lode or blew up on the way. It's Admiral Soddy who wants to know . . ."

"Now that's different! Give that fine man my regards and tell him that his railroad will be completed in seventy-eight hours even if I strip my gears trying!"

"First arse-kissing robot I ever met," the Colonel grunted. "Get onto Soddy and give him the report."

The Admiral greeted the news with enthusiasm, but Parrts had a glazed look in his eyes as he turned off the etherphone.

"He's coming here," Parrts choked.

"So what?"

"He's in orbit now and will be landing in five minutes."

"He's what?!"

The Colonel's eye now had the same glaze. "Got to seal up the torture room, find my class A uniform, get the gold star bedcover for the guest suite, polish the robot reception guard . . . *five minutes!* Get moving, Parrts!"

They made it with thirteen seconds to spare. They stood at attention, the shining squad of robot riflemen behind them, as the ponderous might of the *U.S.E. Insufferable* dropped down through the clouds to the landing pad. The instant it was down, just as the port began to open, Parrts pressed the radio switch hidden in the stripe of his trousers. Instantly music blared out loudly; the Admiral's own theme.

Hail to Soddy, best of all,
Always ready, on the ball.
Never tired, never weary,
Always happy, always cheery.
Always first in peace or war,
Never angry, never sore.

There was more like this, just as obnoxious and untruthful as the opening lines. Greeted in this manner, the Admiral stepped from the port followed by his staff. As he did so Kylling barked an order and the robot riflemen raised their atomic rifles and fired a volley into the air; all except one defective robot who blew the head off the robot next to him. Cursing a vile oath, the Colonel issued another command and all of the other robots turned and fired and disintegrated their erring comrade.

"Still as inefficient as ever, eh Kylling," the Admiral said with a nasty whine.

"Welcome to Strabismus, Admiral Soddy."

"Flayed any good cooks lately, Kylling?"

"A small mistake, sir. He was sent for punishment . . ."

"Punishment did not mean you had to make twelve lampshades out of him. The only good cook I ever found. And get a patch over that bad eye at once. Looking at the so-called good one is bad enough."

"As you command, sir."

"You're damned right! How's my railroad coming?"

At the thought of the railroad the Admiral actually smiled. He was not too unhandsome in a craggy, wrinkled, grey-haired, beady-eyed sort of way. He was also wide-shouldered and trim which did not hurt. With eager tread he stamped over to the track that extended across the bridge to vanish in the tunnel beyond.

"Now that's what I call a hunk of track. Lieutenant Fome – come look at this."

Lt. Fome emerged from the crowd of aides, toadies and lackeys and trotted over to join the Admiral. Parrts, though still rigidly at attention, let his eyes follow her, as did the eyes of all the men there, all pulled over like marbles on a string. With good reason.

Lt. Fome was built like a brick battleship. She didn't walk, she rolled, the ivory columns of her immaculate legs were encased in her spray-on "lustrelight" suit. And each motion of the legs rotated the twin globes of beauty that were her bum. Hair, breasts, lips, nose were all of the same quality, a real great package and a wet slithery sound sounded across the pad as all present licked their lips. This was replaced by a moan of unrequited passion as the Admiral, while explaining to her the finer points of rails and sleeper, pinched her bottom with his free hand.

Even Parrts was impressed – and he enjoyed the unusual sensation. The long months without fending off prospective lovers had restored some of his long-submerged sexual drives. He luxuriated in the novelty until he noticed a pot-bellied commander edging towards him with a certain light in his eye. Depressed again he found little joy in kneeing the commander in the groin. Life was back to its depressing norm.

"All right, stop gaping at the Lieutenant's arse and get the unloading rolling."

His aides scurried to obey. Parrts stepped over the writhing commander and led the surviving robots away. Colonel Kylling's eye widened when he saw the prone form and his empty eyesocket glowed. He took a quick look around and saw that, in the momentary confusion, no one was looking his way. In an instant he had the commander under one anthropoid arm and an even shorter instant later had him through the door and out of sight. A single, weak yelp was cut brutally short. By the time the officer was missed, if he was ever missed, he would be a changed man. And not for the better.

High up on the *Insufferable*'s flank a loading port ground open and a boom slowly extended. Parrts, who was watching curiously, was distracted by someone walking by who stopped suddenly and turned towards him.

Lieutenant Fome. Her eyes widened as she looked at him, the lovely lashes raising like veils from over their beauty. The delicate nostrils flared ever so slightly and the tip of a red tongue flicked out to moisten the full richness of the even redder lips.

"My name is Styreen," a husky, sensuous voice susurrated. "What's yours, handsome."

"Private Parrts, ma'am."

"Yes, I've got them and I hope you have too. You're fast but I like it. Look here."

5
6
target resolution
›MUZZLE PROXIMAL – 3·5 METRES‹
fission discharge!

She slowly opened the closure of her jacket as she spoke and the pink protruberances of her breasts swelled out like twin dirigibles emerging from the same hangar. "Dive in," she husked.

Parrts hands joined together and he swayed forward, ready to plunge into the pool of her passion.

"Fome, stop seducing the troops and get over here." The Admiral's voice cut like a buzz-saw. The dirigibles retreated and the hangar door closed. The rotating rump receded and Parrts blinked and shook his head.

Had it happened? Had he finally reciprocated someone's passion? Indeed he had, and it was quite enjoyable. So *that's* what he had been missing all these years. Yummy!

"You there, Trooper, you with the glazed eyes. Tail onto one of those ropes. I don't want that thing getting banged."

The authority in the Admiral's voice shot Parrts forward to grab the line that dangled near his head. He looked up and gaped at what was on the other end of it.

"A beauty, isn't she," the Admiral enthused. "A perfect replica of a Union Pacific 4-8-8-4 simple-articulated; the biggest steam locomotive ever built. They don't make locomotives that way no more, they don't. Of course there are a few improvements. Such as she's got an atomic engine. But she still gets up a good head of steam for the whistle."

Admiral Soddy was enthusing and chortling and speaking mostly to himself since he greatly loved the sound of his own voice. But Parrts had come closer as he tugged on the line and the Admiral was suddenly aware of his presence.

"Well what have we got here?" he grated. "I gave up this sort of lowerdeck stuff when I made Captain, but for you, baby, I'll make an exception." He pinched a neat cookie of flesh from Parrts's well-scarred buttock. But the dangling engine caught his eye and he was torn between two passions. Being an Admiral he decided to have them both. "Report to my chief of staff. You're assigned to the train. I'll be engineer and you'll be fireman. Won't that be jolly?"

"But I'm assigned to Colonel Kylling, sir."

"You've just been reassigned. Anyway, I saw Kylling slipping off with Paymaster Commander Cash. Kylling won't miss you for quite a while. I won't miss that old bastard either, always whining about finances. It will be an adventure, my boy. Just you and I, and the rest of my staff of course, taking the first train down this fine railroad. Just think of that!"

Parrts thought instead of Lieutenant Fome and the sparkle in his eye matched that of the Admiral's.

"It will be a pleasure to join you, sir. I'll get my bag."

CHAPTER 5.

S
ENCOUN

TRANGE ERS

IT WAS A RATHER UNUSUAL looking train, to say the least. The engine was one of the mighty Union Pacific "Big Boys", gold-plated for extra effect, and the atomic engine it contained was powerful enough to drag a battleship sideways across a mud flat. Next in line came the tender, the pullman cars, fastidious copies of the orignal owned by bank presidents and long-dead tycoons. Dining car, kitchen car, freight cars for supplies, a vista-dome and a caboose to end the thing.

Parrts was impressed. He was even more impressed with Lt. Fome who was conductress of the train and attired in the uniform of her position.

"You make an exotic trainperson," he whispered hoarsely as he bent to inspect a journal behind her.

"You can light my fires anytime, fireman," she velveted in return.

Suddenly Parrts' uniform was too hot, the striped cap restricting, the bibbed overalls confining. He reached to tear them away and the shrill whistle of the train blasted.

"All aboard," Lt. Fome cried, called from Cupid by a sterner duty. "All aboard!" She blew her whistle

OFFICIAL & RESTRICTED
SODDY C.M. EVIDENCE RIGHT SP STEREO PAIR REF STRABL519-LEGAL (W) 'TOWER BRIDGE' RRAGG ERECTED SIMULACRUM
CHARGE NO 15 MISAPPROPRIATION OF FLEET FUNDS

and waved her flag and Parrts cursed and ran to the cab.

"Here we go!" Admiral Engine Driver Soddy screamed and the whistle screeched in echo. "Back her a bit to jam the couplings tight, a touch of sand for the drivers – oh, I've read all the books! – open the throttle and the iron horse lives again!"

"A nutter. A real nutter." Parrts thought gloomily, watching the steam blast out of the cylinders, the smoke roll from the stack. Fake smoke, steam just boiled up for the effect. But all this nonsense would be worth it if he could only lay his lunch-hooks on the lovely Lt. Fome! Styreen, Styreen . . . !

Whistle screeching, wheels rattling, springs squeaking, the mismatched train rumbled across the plateau, clattered across the bridge and vanished into the darkness of the tunnel beyond.

"Good old RRAGG, it's done a fine job," Soddy chuckled as they tore across bridges and roared through tunnels. In a way it was quite exciting and Parrts began to get into the mood of it. In fact, if he could force the memory of Styreen Fome's luscious frame from his fevered brain he found he was actually enjoying this archaic form of transportation.

The air was getting warmer too, as they dropped lower. There was vegetation now in the valleys they crossed, and clear sunshine. Then a tunnel, the longest so far, and the grade flattened and they emerged from the mountain range at last onto the surface of Strabismus. The Admiral bulged his eyes like a wart-hog and clutched his chest as though waiting for the quick blast of a coronary.

"What," he gurgled and gasped, "what's going on here?"

It was very obvious what was going on here. The natives were pouring out of the destroyed city, while the priests in the remains of the temple were urging them on with enthusiasm.

"Back up! Reverse!" Parrts gurgled. "Get us the hell out of here!"

"Never!" Soddy roared. "The schedule will be kept, the mails must go through!" He jammed the throttle forward.

"You're bonkers!" Parrts wailed. "We have no mail, there is no schedule . . ."

His cries were in vain for Soddy was beyond hearing, beyond reason, living in some megalomaniac corner of his twisted synapses. Whistle wailing, steam spouting, they rushed towards certain destruction.

Well, almost certain destruction. The natives were a little on the fragile side and their spears weren't very sharp either. Not only that but they were pretty stupid and had never touched the railroad track. So the train, going faster and faster, hurtled through the centre of the ravaged city, with spears spearing into it and vile alien oaths following the spears. The passengers in the train pressed their faces to the windows with horror at the interesting scenery outside. Then it was gone, vanished in a flash. Except for an occasional passage through a bit of destroyed suburbia or a bisected farm, all was serene again. But the Admiral was taking no chances. He kept the throttle open and the train at full speed until they were well away from the alien civilization they had crunched. A wide river appeared, crossed by a long bridge with the centre span copied after Tower Bridge. Here, far from the shore and possible retribution, Soddy slowed and stopped the train. He put on the brakes and dived for the private car behind. There his doctor plugged him in for a complete blood change and metabolic tune-up while Styreen poured a large glass of Antarean grot-grog on the rocks. With trembling hands he clutched the glass and insufflated half of its poisonous contents.

"Parrts," he gurgled and gasped, *"what* was all that about?"

"Aliens, Admiral. I guess they didn't like what RRAGG did to their city."

"Do you think you can dredge some withered

and dusty explanation from your shrivelled brain as to just *why* RRAGG should have done a thing like that?"

"Yes, sir. He was programmed to treat Strabismus as an uninhabited planet. Despite my insistence that an investigation should be made first," lie, mend a fence, blame the other guy, stay alive, Parrts had been a trooper long enough to learn the drill, "the Colonel and the planetary surveyor insisted on turning the red handle to 'uninhabited.' I did my best, sir."

"I don't believe a word of your smarmy wheedling and after a quick courtmartial all three of you are going to get blown out of an atomic cannon. But meanwhile we have got to get out of this mess. Let's get this thing into reverse and get back."

"I wouldn't advise that, Soddy-baby," Styreen cooed, chucking him under the chin to boost his morale. "I was in the caboose during this dustup and I saw them getting wise a little too late and rolling rocks onto the rails."

"Oh you did, did you, you beady-eyed little devil," he grumbled and slapped at her fingers. "And keep your hands to yourself until we're out of this because I got more to think about at this moment than swapping orgone. Get on the radio and call down a couple of battleships and get me the hell out of here."

"We can't do that, sir," Parrts patiently explained in words of one syllable or less. "In order to keep this train operation authentic timewise we did not bring a radio."

"Whose moronic idea was that?"

"Yours, sir. You thought it a great inspiration at the time."

"Well I thought wrong. Though I'll never admit that. It was your idea, Parrts, and you'll be executed for it as soon as we're out of this mess you got us into. So what can we do?"

"We can go ahead. We have no other choice. One of the tugs that picked up RRAGG will be bringing down the mining machinery and will meet us at the site. They're to lift us off."

"No other way out of this?"

"None, sir."

The Admiral sighed tremulously. "Then that's that. I'm going to slip into my uniform with all the medals. Always a morale booster."

He took off his engine driver's jacket, and with it his shoulders and muscles. With a build like a scrawny chicken, with a pot-belly contained by a girdle, he really wasn't much to look at until the shoulders came back with the uniform jacket. Styreen helped him dress and, behind his back, she rolled her eyes heavenward over his physique – then glanced at Parrts with a burning look. Message received; his body temperature instantly soared twenty degrees above normal and he began to feverishly plot a schedule that involved getting his hands on her for the longest possible time in the quietest possible corner.

"If your mind is on what I think it is on, Parrts, you are ripe for an instant D.D. That means discharged, dead, in military jargon, in case you didn't know."

"I was thinking about the train, sir," he said, but the effect was spoiled by the fact that he squeaked the words in a high falsetto.

"Oh you were, were you. Is that why you are suddenly singing soprano?"

"Worried about those natives, Admiral. A nasty lot." Voice under control at last. "Should I move the train on?"

"No. We're safe enough here – and it's almost dark. We'll depart at the crack of dawn when we can see just what the hell we are driving into. I suppose the odds are good that we might run into – say a few more interesting situations?"

"Well, sir, that old RRAGG is a track-laying fool. You just tell him go and he goes . . ."

"All right. I got the message. Get my staff in here and we'll see about guards during the night. And get my chef because he has to whip up something special to take my mind off my problems. Lt. Fome you can help there too. Get into one of those black transparent things after dinner and lay on a kilo of hash and a couple of pipes and we really will forget out troubles . . ."

It was the word "troubles" that did it. Barely had the fatal word slipped from the Admiral's sordid lips than the troubles arrived.

There was a heavy thud on the roof of the coach followed instantly by shrill screaming from the next car. Parrts rushed to the window while the Admiral dived under the table.

"What is it?" he croaked.

"Flying creatures, sir, with other nasty-looking aliens riding them. They're dive-bombing the train.."

"With *bombs*?"

"No, sir, with crap. It might be more accurate to say they are dive-crapping us . . ."

"Stick your damn grammar lessons, Parrts! Why us?"

"They come from that direction, sir, the way the track goes . . ."

"Shut up!" the Admiral implied.

"The attack's over, sir. They're flapping off. I'll check for damage."

"You do that while Lt. Fome pours the rest of that bottle into my glass."

The damage was slight, although the train looked like a statue that had been a hundred years in the park.

The guards, the ones who had been outside, had thrown their uniforms into the river and, after bathing, had been sedated for shock. They could have died. It would have been a crappy way to go. Darkness dropped its ebony cloak, but other things dropped as well since there was now a fine bomber's moon to illuminate the scene. Parrts rose to the occasion and, risking a cloacal concussion, armoured only by a raincoat and umbrella, made it to the engine and fired her up. Once the train was moving it made aiming difficult and they rumbled away through the night until the dark and welcome embrace of a tunnel mouth loomed up in the headlight ahead and the train slunk into its welcome embrace.

Despite his fatigue, Parrts having taken a quick shower rushed back through the train only to discover that the Admiral, stoned and drunk, had passed out. But he had locked Styreen in with him before clunking to the floor and Parrts kicked the door with rage. Styreen kicked back, filled with the same emotions. They had a good kick, which accomplished nothing, so she went to sleep and he went to the dining car, strangely empty after the trying day, and ate the Admiral's dinner which was very good indeed.

At the hour of dawn, porters, lowly lieutenants drafted for the job, went through and woke everyone up. The lowest rating aboard, the second dishwasher, volunteered to scout ahead – after they had bandaged him – and came back to report that nothing was visible outside the tunnel. The Admiral, restored by his rest, and two more complete changes of blood, seized the throttle and they were away again.

The mighty engine pulled them effortlessly through a peaceful countryside, hour after hour of it. The sun shone warmly, then it rained for a bit – which was fine since the train needed a washing – then it hailed, which added a necessary scouring action. Admiral Soddy sang an old railroad song, very jolly, all about burst boilers and scalded bodies, and sent back for lobster sandwiches and champagne.

"This is the life, hey, fireman," he exulted. "Simple food, the open iron road, not a care in the world . . ."

They hurtled around a bend to see that the narrow valley ahead was completely blocked by a high stone wall that went right across the tracks.

U.S.E.

CHAPTER 6.

ST
ALLIAN

TRANGE

ICES

THE BRAKES LOCKED, full on, under the Admiral's hysterical command. There was a fascinating cacophony as all the wheels on all the cars slid on the solid steel, screeching and howling. There was a good deal of this inside the train as well, as people hurtled to the floor, had heavy things fall on them, had hot soup decanted on their ankles and so forth.

In the cab, driver and fireman, wished they were Admiral and Trooper again as the solid wall loomed closer and closer, larger and larger, until they could see the rough surface of the rocks, the lines of mortar between them. They were slowing, the wall was getting closer, until they hit . . . and stopped with the smallest of crunching sounds.

"I think we broke our headlight," Parrts quavered.

"Reverse! out of here!" the Admiral quavered as well, as the first arrows thudded into the engine's gold plate surrounding them. A happy screaming sounded from the wall above and a few large rocks joined the arrows.

They reversed as far as the bend. They were not followed. Now that he was safe, anger replaced fear in the Admiral's gaze and he drained the champagne and threw the bottle at the wall; it fell short. He then hurled dirty old military curses at the barrier. The passengers, bloodied and soup-stained, ran up crunchily on the ballast and gaped at the blockade.

"What will we *do*?" an ensign wailed.

"Have that coward shot," the Admiral responded instantly. "No, wait, he is volunteering to lead the attack on the wall."

Fear of imminent death instantly doubled the ensign's I.Q. and he produced a brilliant alternative plan.

"Instead of an attack, Admiral, which I would be pleased to lead, but might not get us past the wall, which looks rather solid, why don't we just burn the wall down with lasers? That would have the dual advantage of also burning down whatever is hurling those spears."

"Talk fast, boy, the sands of your time are running out."

"Aye, aye, sir! You see I was in charge of loading the right of way maintenance supplies that you ordered. We have sleepers, track, bolts, tools, everything we might need in case of washouts or things fallen on the track . . ."

"There's something fallen on *this* track all right!"

"In addition to those, we also have construction lasers. Not as strong as battle lasers but powerful enough to burn that thing out of the way."

"Agreed. Five men of my bodyguard to guard your body – and the laser – and get moving. Start at the top and bring her down course by course. Cut off before you burn out the rails and we'll move off the bottom layer by hand. Go."

They went, and it was a satisfactory operation in every way. They stayed out of range of the arrows and began burning to the accompaniment of shrill alien screams. A sortie by the enemy, who looked a good deal like the pilots of yesterday's *merde*-birds, was easily shot down by the blasters of the bodyguards. Depressed by this failure the aliens were gone long before their wall was. Then, sweating at the unaccustomed effort, the troopers levered the last of the boulders off the rails which were now bent, twisted over and generally battered around.

"Goody," Admiral Soddy said when he came up to inspect – after patrols had cleared the area for a kilometre in every direction. "We are going to have to lay a bit of track. Just the way they did it in the good old days. No power aids here! I'll make gandy-dancers out of you yet."

The Admiral was as good as his word. If only he had been as good an admiral as he was a rail-buff the war might have been won years earlier. The old rails were unbolted, the ballast firmed and levelled, the sleepers aligned, fresh rails brought up by grunting troopers with great pincers, fishplates slapped on and bolted into place. All under the Admiral's instructions, if not with his physical aid.

"Now that wasn't too bad, was it?" he asked, sipping a cool drink under the shade of an umbrella, smiling down at the prostrate and sun-burned forms that littered the ground on all sides. "You all have my thanks – and a free beer each with dinner to demonstrate the depths of my generosity. Now let's get this show on the road."

Like zombies the corpses rose and shuffled aboard the train. The whistle blew and off they went. Parrts looked out gloomily at the scenery as it sailed by and wondered how all this madness would end. In a nasty death, he was sure. The train was chuffing through a tangled forest now, tooting loudly on the turns, sending flocks of small flying lizards winging away wildly at the sound. Parrts eyed them suspiciously since they looked very much like miniaturized versions of the turd-attackers of the night before. His suspicions were unhappily justified as they swept out of the forest into rolling countryside under cultivation. Occasional farm buildings began to zip by and, in the fields, lizardoids pulled the ploughshares, while even nastier looking green-skinned things guided the ploughs. They shook their farm tools at the train and threw clods of dirt as it hurtled by.

"Ha-ha, stupid greenies," the Admiral discriminated. "Stone Age morons. Bet they turn red with jealousy when they see this fine product of a superior culture."

"Stone Age is sure the right word, Admiral. That was a pretty neat stone wall they built across the tracks."

"Are these the same creeps?"

"They are. And they organized those bombing runs as well. They are bifurcated lizardoid reptilia with dentation . . ."

"I'm going to shoot you for a spy, Parrts. You talk too smart for a simple trooper . . ."

"I am too smart to be a simple trooper, dear kind Admiral. I am an exobiologist forcefully drafted by malice – "

"Is there any other way anyone is drafted?" the

Admiral asked, shocked at the thought. "So practice your exobiology and tell me what all that is coming up."

"Villages giving way to towns, a sort of reptilian suburbia complete with crocodile-drawn coaches, gardens with gnomes. I would hazard a guess that all this will soon metamorph into a large urban conurbation . . ."

"Say 'city', I can take it. And knowing the past record of that track-laying moron RRAGG this railroad is going to bash right through it."

"Correct, sir. You do have remarkable intelligence for someone holding so high a rank. If you would just begin braking now you will see this city coming up around the next bend."

It was very impressive indeed; everything a large and prosperous city should be, except for the fact that it had a nasty length of railroad track crunched right down through the middle of it. The track was intact this time. But a certain reception had been prepared. As they slid to a smooth stop outside the walls the Admiral choked out his words.

"Are you seeing what I am seeing?"

"I am, if you are seeing down there in the middle of the city a spike on the tracks as big as a scoutship that will impale this engine if we keep going."

"And when we are stopped all those towers next to the tracks will dump rocks and burning oil and such on top of us. We gotta lay track around this dump, bypass it completely."

"Negative, Admiral. Firstly, we don't have enough track. Secondly, even if we did I doubt if we could lay it under fire. Thirdly . . ."

"Thirdly, smart-ass, I should have shot you before I ever met you. You got me into this mess . . ."

"Perhaps, sir" Parrts smarmed. "But if I did then I will get you out. Do you have an exolinguist on your staff?"

"Of course."

"Then we will parley. Talk to these aborigines. Strike a deal, sell them beads, give them war reparations."

"We could fight!"

"We could lose and be eaten alive by gaping lizard jaws filled with rotting fangs . . ."

"Send up the exolinguist!" the Admiral screamed into the intercom. "And a large white flag, with my initials in gold in the corner, on a flagpole. And snap to it."

Within short minutes Lt. Fome appeared, proudly marching with the Admiral's banner of defeat. Parrts tore his eyes away from her manifold attractions and looked over her shoulder. "Where is the exolinguist?" he asked.

"I am she" she said.

"Darling," Parrts slobbered, instantly shrinking five centimetres as his knees turned to jelly, "an exquisite body and a brain . . ."

"Parrts, you oversexed simpleton!" bellowed the Admiral, "delay that horny stuff until your next shore leave. Get out there with the Lieutenant and talk us out of this, do you hear? As encouragement I promise to raise you to lance-corporal if you succeed. As further encouragement I want to assure you that a telescopic rifle will be trained on you at all times and you will be shot the instant you fail."

"With you as my C.O. who needs an enemy?" Parrts sighed. "Come, Lieutenant, we go to our destiny."

He took the flag from her and they marched stolidly forward down the tracks. Their hands met, held, and a powerful current zipped from flesh to flesh.

"Styreen," he lachrymosed.

"Parrts," she responded.

"Should we, here?"

"Darling, of course."

"The ballast won't be too rough?"

"What will be too rough will be going another instant without . . ."

"ALL RIGHT, YOU TWO!" the amplified voice of the Admiral boomed out. "NO ORGIES FOR THE NATIVES' BENEFIT. KEEP WALKING."

They paced ever closer, walking ever slower, stopping when a shower of arrows thudded down before them.

"Peace!" Parrts shouted, waving the flag rapidly. "Paz, pace, pax! Styreen sweetie, could you do your exolingual thing and chat them up about our good intentions."

"I would, my only sugar-plum, but what language should I talk to them in? By hypnojection I speak 657 languages. Would you know which one they might speak here?"

"Probably none of them," Parrts muttered, edging closer and looking at the scowling hordes of the enemy. "Since this is our first contact I don't see how they could speak any of the known galactic languages. Though these creatures resemble the Hestkooians, they have the dental work of the Vaskebjorn."

"I speak both of those," she said brightly.

"Of course, my precious, but neither is going to work here – AHHAA!"

"I squeezed your hand too hard?" she worried.

"Never! Crush me, consume me, yummm. yumm . . ." He shook his head fuzzily. "What was I saying?"

"You said AHHHAA!"

"Yes, I did, didn't I, but why . . . ? *Yes,* I remember! Look, there, on top of the wall, with the chain around its neck. Isn't that a Gornishthilfen?"

"The thing that looks like a broken lobster with too many claws?"

"The very one!"

"I don't know. I've never seen one, though of course I speak Gornishthilfen like a native." She shivered deliciously. "Though of course I would not like to look like one."

"Never! The exoskeleton . . ." Parrts pulled himself together abruptly as an arrow bounced off his left boot. "Speak to it at once. We must open communication."

"Ĉu vi audas min?" she shouted, waving to the creature. *"Ni estas amikog kaj deziras paroli . . ."*

"Ekmortu, filino de hundino, forniku vin ankaŭ!"

"What did it say?" Parrts asked.

"Good morning, how are you?"

"The lizards didn't seem to think so. They're giving it a good touch of the spear and a twist of the chain. Colonel Kylling would have liked to see this."

"I'll try again."

The Gornishthilfen did not really want to talk to them, but the lizardoids knew enough of his language to tell when he was just being insulting and the crunch of spear on shell soon convinced him to co-operate. The humans inched forward, eyeing the weapons around them unhappily, and a parley soon began.

"We come in peace" Styreen said.

"Not bloody likely," the creature rattled, "even these stupid lizards can see what your machine has done to their city."

"Just tell them it was an accident, a badly-programmed piece of machinery. We are willing to pay reparations, supply blankets and elastoplast to the wounded, and large bribes to officials."

The lizards were naturally suspicious and, for some reason, were not interested in any of the bribes or offers.

"But they must want something," Parrts whispered in Styreen's shell-like ear, "or they would not be talking to us like this."

"We'll find out soon," she re-whispered in return. "I have been eavesdropping when this crunchy creature talks to the lizards and I think I know their language well enough now to talk to them directly."

"My, but you learn fast!"

"That's not the only thing I'm fast . . ."

"I can see and hear everything," the Admiral's

voice boomed weakly from the distant train. "Get on with it."

"Honourable King Kroakr," Styreen gurgled in the local excuse for a language, "we offer friendly aid to you and your lovely green people."

"You speak Slimian?" the King asked with surprise, his eyes shooting out on stalks.

"I have just learned it now, listening to you talk to this creature."

"Well good for you, sweetie," he turned and shouted to the guards. "Into the pot with that thing and it's lobster soup for all for dinner."

The troops cheered and the Gornishthilfen shouted wicked oaths as it slid down the chute into the waiting boiling water. The King turned back and smiled at Styreen, most impressively too with three rows of sharp red teeth. "Then you're ready to make a deal?"

"Whatever you say, King. That's what we're here for. We really didn't mean to crunch you nice city . . ."

"Think nothing of it. For the most part your machine went through the prole neighbourhoods and did a bit of inadvertent city planning for us. When those tracks come up I'm going to have a nice new royal mile. But there is one thing we want, are you willing to grant it?"

"I am but a simple girl translator with no powers to act but will relay your message to my commanding officer, Admiral Soddy."

"Well relay me to him instead, I don't talk to no hired hands. And the first thing I want you to relay to him is that the track behind your train is now torn up, and if so much as one of my claws is harmed you will all be killed and eaten. Let's go."

The Admiral, who had been following the conversation by spy-ray got the idea pretty quickly. Parrts and Lt. Fome led the parade back, with the white flag at half-mast, followed by an honour guard around King Kroakr who was carried in a gilt throne borne by six king-sized lizards. By the time they reached the train a marquee had been set up, champagne set out in buckets, and – having seen a little of the King's gustatory delights – a number of cold lobsters were arranged on plates.

"This is the Slimian King Krokr," Lt. Fome said when the two groups were within eyeball contact.

"You can say that again! Slimey is the word."

"That's the name of his country, Admiral."

"Wonderful. I'm really glad to see him. Translate that."

The King pulled his eyeballs back in. "Them's mighty small crustacea," he said. "Translate that."

"Small but tasty. Try one." The Admiral wrenched off a claw, delicately forked out the meat and chomped it. The King watched all this with extended eye stalks, then grabbed up the largest lobster of all, flipped it into the air and opened his mouth. The humans all stepped back a pace, since it was like looking into a tooth-lined tunnel. The lobster dropped, the jaws snapped shut, there was a quick crunch and a gulp and the King reached for a couple more.

"As you say, small but tasty, Admiral. Now let's get down to work. Your machine devastated my city, ploughed up my countryside, killed a couple of hundred of my citizens and generally screwed up the works around here for a good time to come."

"Accidents happen, King."

"I'm sure they do. But I'm going to forget about all the things that have happened and let this train choo-choo on to wherever the hell it is going and in return for this immense favour you are going to do one little weensy favour for me."

"Anything, Kingy, you have but to ask."

"Settled then. We go to war against the enemy tomorrow. With you and your troops in the van we will wipe them out. Pass the champers to wash these things down."

CHAPTER 7. BAL
ATTA

LOON
CK

TWO OFFICERS HELD THE ADMIRAL bent over while a third pounded lustily on his back to get the pieces of lobster out of his throat and to stop his coughing. All of the Slimians watched this with fascination, eyeballs at full stalk. Parrts and Styreen, unnoticed by the Admiral for the first time since they had met, instantly vanished between the coaches and had the fastest knee-trembler in the history of military forces. The Admiral straightened up, red-faced and gasping, the eye stalks detumesced, as did Parrts and Styreen who emerged, hand in hand, eyeballs damply aswim with love.

"Did you say war?" the Admiral rasped and croaked hoarsely.

"He should learn Slimian," the King said. "He's already got a very good accent. And, yes, those were my very words."

"Against who?"

"Them! Those! The edible enemy! The Gornishthilfen who dropped from the sky in ships of fire and have since been giving me the old squeeze and trying to boot me out of my own country."

"Can anyone tell me just what this crappy crocodile is talking about?" the Admiral whined, still huskily.

Parrts stepped forward and saluted, feeling ten feet tall, ready to lick his weight in Barsoomian bobcats. "The Gornishthilfen were one of the first races contacted in the expansion of our co-prosperity sphere. They were not interested in being civilized or co-prosperited. The war against them was long and deadly. In the end, since they would not see the merit of our argument, we hit their home planet with a parking-lot bomb. Melted everything on the surface right down two kilometres deep. Planet's got a great albedo now!"

"So we knocked them out. So how come they're here?"

"They never surrendered, not even when the lava was closing over their heads. None of their bases surrendered either and all had to be knocked off one by one. We're still finding them on lost and distant planets."

"And this is about as lost and distant as any of them."

"Right you are, sir, hidden right under our very noses. Looks like some of them came here and are trying to take over from the locals."

"How many are there?"

"That's what we'll have to find out, won't we, sir."

Soddy sipped champagne and thought, and the ruddy colour seeped down below his collar and out of his fingertips. Then he spoke.

"We're going to help you knock off these bums, King. Then you can have your nice country back and we can get the hell out of this dump. But we gotta look first, see how they are set-up, make plans."

"Sure," the King said, gulping as he polished off the last lobster. "Take all the time you want. Take a whole day. Meanwhile my boys will be on guard here. Try to pull any fast ones, fatty, and I'll have you for lunch." They reared back as he laughed, jaws wide, and the smell of olde swamp washed over them.

It was a small reconnaissance party. Parrts, as the exobiologist historian, went to see what was up, Lt. Fome went to translate, and the MP Major went to keep them out of the sack together. What surprised them was their mode of transportation.

"A balloon!" Parrts gaped.

"No jokes, buddy," the pilot snarled, clashing an impressive number of teeth. "You're not in the boonies now. We're civilized. We got balloons, flush toilets, ballpoint pens, french-fried worms and a lot of things you never heard of in the swamp you came from."

"Whee!" Parrts muttered. "Styreen, darling, will you tell this hair-triggered lizard I meant no offence. If I meet any other crocodiles I'll send them here. The place really swings. Now, can we get on with our little sightseeing expedition?"

With guttural Slimian cries the balloon was launched and the pilot, with a shout of command, started the engine. The galley-slaves bent to their task, the propeller spun, and they soared majestically above the rooftops.

"If I hadn't a seen it I wouldn't a believed it," Parrts muttered, eyeballs wide at this miracle of transportation. He tried to give Styreen a crafty pinch but the ever-alert MP Major got him on the knuckles with the butt of his gun. Sucking his fingers Parrts stared, with little relish, at the fortified plateau that was coming into view ahead.

"That's it," their pilot said. "I'm not going too close because they got some wicked AA defences. Flame guns, stuff like that. So we're stuck in a stand-off. As long as they're up there we can't touch them. But even lousy lobsters gotta eat so they make

raids on our farms and that's when we have some fancy dust-ups. They got us outgunned, but we have them outmanned. The slave battalions go in first to soak up the casualties, then we follow with the shock troops, ballistae, poo-bombers, the works." He looked glum, about as glum as a green Saurian can look. "Only it usually doesn't work too well and we take a beating. But that's gonna change now we got you aliens with your big guns. You make a hole in their defences, we tear through it and there is a big lobster feed for all!"

"Tell me," Parrts asked, "do you want to wipe out the enemy – or eat them?"

The pilot gave Parrts a wicked smile, with plenty of evil teeth showing, and a slow wink with his nictitating membrane. At the same moment a gout of flame filled the air before them and he kicked the balloon into a tight turn.

"The defences look pretty rough here," the Major said, eyeing the ranked gun emplacements gloomily. "Let's try the other side."

"Looks maybe better on this side," Parrts said, as they swung about in a slow circle. "The jungle comes right up the cliff – and it's a bit lower..."

"Look out!" Styreen screamed prettily, then rescreamed the warning in six more languages before she sound the right Slimian scream.

The pilot banked sharply into a turn, or as sharply as his prehistoric means of transportation would allow, and they all had a good view of the flying robot tearing towards them, ridden by one of the hideous Gornishthilfen. The slaves began turning the propeller like crazy as the enemy got off a blast with its flame rifle. Everyone else was pretty much screaming and falling about except for the MP Major, who was a career sadist and liked killing people and things, who levelled his gun, held his fire until the range was right and then let off a single blast that got the robot right between the eyes. It began smoking and giving off sparks and little cogwheels as it spiralled down towards the trees below, its alien rider shaking its claws at them angrily as it fell.

"Great shot," Parrts said.

"So was the lobster's," the pilot growled. "Got our gasbag and we're going down. If I wasn't cold-blooded I'd be sweating right now. We've got to get clear of the jungle before we hit."

Despite the ferocious cranking of the slaves, they didn't. With a great cracking of branches, human and Saurian screams, the balloon broke its way down through the trees, spilling them all out into the waiting thorn bushes below.

"Our trenches are this way!" the pilot cowardly cried and led the retreat.

"Too late," the MP Major said happily, shooting down an attacking Gornishthilfen, "they are upon us. But I am going to take a battalion of these crummy crabs with me before I go."

It was a running battle, and a confused one in amongst the creepers and trees, with screams, groans, crunches and shots on all sides. Parrts pulled Styreen after him, then had to stop and fight as an attacking wave of shelled shock-troops broke over them. It looked like the end until a counter-attack from the trenches came over the top and swept all before it. And all the time he was fighting Parrts never once let go of Styreen's gloved hand.

"Touch and go for a while there," he phewed, then looked at the glove and discovered there was no longer a hand in it. "My love!" he wailed and dived back to the attack where he was tackled by the MP Major.

"Hold it, buddy, because this is maybe the break we need. Aliens always gotta take screaming busty girls captives – you've seen the covers of the propaganda magazines. And they always carry them off. So we follow and see what secret tunnel they take her into, the one from which they emerged for this attack. Right?"

"Right." Parrts nodded agreement – then pointed

behind the Major. "But they're attacking again!"

The Major wheeled about and Parrts got him neatly behind the ear with the butt of his pistol. Then, jumping over him even as he fell and ignoring the cries of the Slimians, he dived into the jungle to rescue his beloved. In the distance he could hear the crashings of the enemy accompanied by the screams of an Earth girl facing a fate worse then death. Ignoring the thorns and brittle branches he rushed after them, grating terrible oaths as he went.

Then all was suddenly silent, except for the usual screams, cries, grunts and plop-plops that were normal to the jungle, and his heart sank in a coronary crash-dive. Was he too late?

Unhappily, he was too late. When he emerged from the jungle he found only a grassy strip with the solid rock wall of the plateau beyond. He prowled along the base, looking for some chink or clue, alternately cursing with anger, then groaning with despair. For what must have been hours he searched, but with no luck. He returned to the spot where he had broken out of the jungle, and sat on a log, his head in his hands, fighting against the blackness of lost love that threatened to overwhelm him. Alas! Alas!

A sudden rattling rumble penetrated his despair. With a stifled glad cry he leapt to his feet, gun ready. A section of the apparently solid stone was swinging open like a door, just like it did in all the bad movies. This was his chance. He would blast them as they emerged, then sneak inside and rescue his darling. The first evil, vicious, foul, alien head appeared and he fired. Luckily he wasn't a very good shot.

"Well, some big welcome, I'm sure," Styreen pouted, brushing the new parting that had been seared in her lovely hair.

"My darling, my precious, I didn't know, forgive me!" he grovelled and kissed her singed locks. "Arrgh! I'll kill this one!"

He raised his gun to destroy the lobsterish form emerging from the cavern behind her and she karateyed his wrist so the gun dropped from his numb fingers.

"Listen, stupid, enough already. If you will notice the chains on its claws and the chain around its neck, the other end of which ends in my little pink hand, you will possible figure out what is happening even with your shrinking brain."

"How . . . what . . .?" he gurgled.

"I'll explain, but could we please do it on the run? They'll be after us soon." As they trotted along, booting the Gornishthilfen before them, she said, "When they captured me I knew what was up, having seen the magazine covers. I screamed nicely and my jacket got torn so my boobs showed and all the usual. They took me to King Crab here who leered and clutched at me, scream as I would, but I explained I never got involved in exobiological miscegenation with an audience since I would barely watch it myself. So he said okay and got rid of the audience and I gave him the old one, two, twist."

"What's that? A new kind of judo?"

"No, culinary cunning. I used to work in a fish restaurant cleaning crustaces. After that you know what happened..."

"Dive aside, I've got him in my sights, I'll blow him to crabdom come!"

"Shut up, Major," she ordered, haughtily imperious, as the MP popped up. "This enemy is my prisoner. If you will look close you will see the stars riveted to its shell which indicates it is of the highest rank. We will take it back and torture it..."

"I can help," Parrts said eagerly. "I learned a lot from the Colonel."

". . . and it will reveal the secrets of the fortifications and we will attack and win."

All of the Slimians accompanying the Major shouted with joy and carried them in triumph back to the train.

CHAPTER 8.

& DOUBLE-

"WELL, WELL, AND WHAT do we have here?" Admiral Soddy said, leaning back in the padded luxury of his private car, smoking a large cigar well stuffed with hash.

"We have the old double-cross," the Gornishthilfen prisoner said in perfect English, rattling its claws so the imprisoning chains fell to the floor.

"No one move," Styreen snapped, her ready gun covering them all. "Pull down the shades and lock the door so the Slimians don't see what is happening." They jumped to obey the imperious order of the flame-scarred muzzle of her gun. "That's better." She put the gun away and fluffed her hair and sighed. "What a day it has been."

"Would you like to explain what is happening before I throttle you?" the Admiral hinted.

"Aye, aye, sir. This lobsteroid is Hummer, the commanding officer of the troops here. He came up with an offer we can't refuse."

"You bet I did," Hummer said, sniffing the air. "Could I have one of those doped stogies before I go on? It's been a long day." The Admiral handed him one and he ate it. "Yum. Well it goes like this. Those lizards out there are as bent as a hairpin and have been feeding you a line. After my unit escaped from the benevolent genocide of you terrestrial monsters we fled to this planet to preserve our ancient, peaceful culture that you were hell-bent on destroying. We hid out here, right under your noses where we knew you would be too stupid to find us, and got along well with the natives except for these Slimians who just want one thing. We offered them art, painting, science. They offered us the cooking pot. They now have us surrounded and we can't break out and sooner or later we end up on the menu which is why I'm offering you this deal."

"No deals," the Admiral snapped. "We already have a deal with the Slimians and as soon as we settle your hash we push on and off this lunatic planet for ever."

CROSS

CROSS

"Fat chance. As soon as you help them put paid to us they grab you, nationalize your railroad, and you follow us through the kitchen. They'll eat anything."

"Got any better offers?" the Admiral asked weakly, puffing so rapidly on his cigar that the end burst into flame and flared like a torch.

"You betcha." Hummer whipped the flaming cigar from the Admiral's limp fingers and popped it into his mouth. Smoke leaked out through joints in his shell as he talked. "Take a look at this plan." He withdrew a map from an orifice in his carapace. "You see your train tracks go through this patch of jungle here, and more jungle leads up this valley there to a low spot on our plateau. What you do is tell the lizards to break the rail line in the woods and secretly lay track right up the valley. Then you suggest to them that you come belting down the track and into the woods but, instead of coming out the other side, you tear up the valley in your Big Boy loco, guns blasting, and shoot a hole through our defences. The Slimians then pour through the gap and, guess who's coming for dinner. At the same time they will have launched a little fake attack on the other side but really all their forces are here and they can't lose. And the train can't get away because the track only leads to the plateau."

"That's really a great idea," the Admiral exclaimed, his words dripping with sarcasm," . . . for them. It looks like you and us end up in the same pot."

"Wrong. That is where the old double-cross comes in. Because as soon as *they* lay the track up the valley *we* lay a looped track back through the jungle *away* from the valley, hooking up with your mainline here, and we put in a secret switch here. The scenario will then go like this: you come belting up the valley, all guns blazing, with the chameleon cavalry right behind you. The switch is thrown and you vanish into the jungle, re-appear on the other side and go tearing away from them for ever. They are so pissed-off they take off after you, but can't catch you, and while they are in pursuit we are down the other side and well away before they know it."

"It looks good," the Admiral said slowly, going over the plan in his mind, then flashing a red-eyed look of suspicion at Hummer, "but how do we know we can trust you?"

"You don't, you grey-skinned bulbous bag of lard!" Hummer screamed, snapping his claws in anger. "But it's the only crap game in town. If you don't like it, stay in that dead-end valley and see your chances are of not ending up as the meat course with some Saurian salad. We *want* you to get away, dummy. You're the diversion that gives us the chance to give them the slip. Now take five minutes to give yourselves all the rationalizations that will enable you to go along with it, then we will get down to the nitty-gritty of planning." Hummer grabbed a clawful of cigars from the humidor, chomped on them

viciously, then went and sat in the corner, antennae semaphoring with annoyance.

"We have to do it," Parrts said. "And we can believe old Hummer there because, until we destroyed them, the Gornishthilfen were the most cultured, courteous, civilized, honest race we ever encountered."

"You don't make us sound too good," the Admiral snorted.

"We're not. So let's stop playing with ourselves and get the ball rolling and get out of here."

Naturally the Slimians agreed to the plan, chortling behind their pallid paws with evil glee at this great chance for a two-course dinner. They even carried the rails and sleepers into the jungle to help the humans lay track. Nor did they grumble about carrying a large box labelled "RAILROAD SUPPLIES" that rattled when it was lifted and contained you-know-who. Under the cover of night Hummer scuttled back to his plateau, through the secret door of course, and everyone crossed their fingers and had a good drink to forget their troubles.

The morning dawned fine, the troops were at their stations, and the two commanders of the attacking forces met for the last time before the battle.

"It is sure good to work with a gentleman," Admiral Soddy said with the utmost insincerity.

"And of course the same goes for you," King Kroakr responded in his most oily manner. They shared a lobster and a bottle of wine and clapped each other on the back and swore eternal brotherhood.

"And that is the last I hope I ever see of that bastard," the Admiral said in the direction of the retreating back.

"That human comes pre-stuffed with lobster," Kroakr confided in an aide, "and I want him for my very own. Let the battle begin."

Horns sounded feebly from the other side of the plateau followed by the tinny clash of weapons from the diversionary forces. Meanwhile the massed might of the Slimian army was concealed in the jungle, ready for the surprise attack. Aboard the train all was in readiness, steam up and neutrons sizzling through the atomic pile. All of the lasers had been mounted on the roofs, ready to fire, and weapons projected from the windows. Even the cook had his biggest cleaver clutched in his hand, for some stupid reason known only to himself. Ahead, at the city's edge, a green form appeared and waved a red flag back and forth three times.

"The signal! Let's go!"

With utmost stealth the mighty engine chugged forward, through the city and under the threatening towers that threatened no more, around the plateau and under the trees, where the track bent off into the jungle. King Kroakr was waiting there, at the head of his forces, and he waved and smiled at the Admiral at the controls of his now battered and grimy engine.

"See you in the pot," Kroakr smirked under his breath, still smiling.

"I'm gonna come back and make a suitcase out of you," the Admiral muttered, smiling just as broadly as they rattled by.

The moment of truth. Breaths were held as they puffed up the valley past the leading lines of the attackers and around the last bend, to the spot where a buffer marked the end of the track.

"We've been had!" the Admiral cried, jamming on the brakes.

"No!" Parrts cried, equally as loud, knocking Soddy's hand from the controls.

Closer and closer they rolled, the Admiral muttering over his sore wrist, and just as Parrts himself was reaching dispiritedly for the brake a crab-like form stepped out from behind a tree and threw a concealed switch. The light turned green, they rattled across the points and the switchman waved them on.

"Let her rip!" the Admiral roared as he jammed the throttle on.

There were a lot of gaping jaws in the Slimian army that day. Their plan was working perfectly, the machine of their soon-to-be-consumed allies was chuffing along nicely into the box canyon as planned – when suddenly with a blasting roar the great engine accelerated, appeared to veer off the track and with the entire train vanished into the jungle. King Kroakr almost croaked as the caboose swung into the trees and was gone.

"What on Strabismus is going on?" he gnashed, bits of splintered teeth flying in all directions. The Saurian army slithered to a stop, not knowing what would happen next – until a balloon scout soared in low and reported that the train was escaping. Revenge? The attackers turned at a sharp right angle and took off after their fleeing prisoners.

In the Union Pacific Big Boy the Admiral was congratulating himself on the brilliance of his plan. "We really did it," he chortled, "fooled the lot of them. Got clean away."

"They don't seem to like the idea." Parrts suggested, leaning out of the cab and looking back at the hordes of running, riding, flying, slithering, and angry Slimians that had erupted from the jungle hard on their trail.

"Don't worry," the Admiral sneered, "they'll never catch us!"

They roared around a bend and saw that a pile of nice big rocks was heaped on the tracks. Once again brakes locked and they banged and screeched to a halt, close enough to read the sign on the rock pile.

> YOU DON'T WANT TO GET TOO FAR AHEAD OF THE PURSUING HORDES. IT'LL TAKE A FEW MINUTES TO MOVE THESE ROCKS WHICH WILL ENCOURAGE THE SLIMIANS TO FOLLOW YOU, NOT US. BETTER GET CRACKING!
>
> TRULY YOURS, HUMMER.

"Get cracking!" the Admiral commanded and set a fine example to the troops by leaping from the cab and tugging at the nearest boulder. "Everyone out!" Parrts shouted, and joined him.

They put their backs into it, greatly encouraged by the approaching hordes already gurgling victorious gurgles. The leading balloons and poo-bombers were already dropping their loads on the train before the last boulder was rolled aside, and the sweating troopers were barely able to grab onto the train as it lurched forward. Saurian claws scrabbled at the caboose, now looking very much like a porcupine with all their arrows sticking from it.

"If you don't pay, you don't ride," Conductress Fome said sweetly, stamping on the last clutching paws until the Slimians released their hold and went slithering in the dust. Now the cries of victory turned to moans of failure as the train picked up speed, faster and faster down the line. The attacking army slowed and stopped. No one waved bye-bye. Styreen did, but doubted if they appreciated the gesture. Then the enemy began milling about – reports of the ruse must have reached the King – and then tore off back in the direction from which they had come.

"And good riddance," Styreen said, and without being asked, cracked out a chilled bottle of champagne and brought it forward to the engine.

"You are too kind," Parrts said damply.

"About time," the Admiral said dustily, spitting sand from his lips, then quaffing an immense tankard of bubbly.

The farms had given way to rolling plains, the plains grew drier and more arid until they found themselves traversing an apparently endless desert of yellow sand.

"Pretty flat," Parrts said, "but there is a tunnel coming up in that black hill ahead."

Styreen looked up and screamed. "That's no tunnel it's a . . ." She fainted and Parrts caught her.

Modus
Optic
Autozoom
144 ms
15
MEM
RAD

ALL CH

CHAPTER 9.

IANGE

THEY GROUND TO A HALT. The Admiral looked with unconcealed horror at the giant black and loathsome form that lay across the track. Big as a small hill, surrounded by obscenely hairy legs, its mouth a gaping maw as big as a tunnel into which the railroad tracks vanished. "What *is* that thing?"

"I, as a simple private, have no idea," Parrts said in a moronic other-ranks voice, rubbing Styreen's limp wrists.

"You told me you were an exobiologist!"

"How could a private be an exobiologist?" he said, trickily. "Your unconscious exolinguist here is a lieutenant."

"Wise guy, huh?" I'll have you shot for this yet. Bend thy knee, Private, rise Lieutenant."

"Aye, aye, sir!" Parrts whipped some gold bars from his pocket, pinned them on and snapped to attention. "I recognize that creature."

"Oh you do do you, you blackmailing son of a bitch. What is it?"

"One of the most formidable life forms ever discovered. You have heard of the loathsome dune-roller, haven't you?"

"Yes."

"Well this one is worse. This is the dune-buggy. It appears to be able to cross interstellar space in egg form and hatches whenever it lands on a desert planet. Its chitin is laser proof. It eats metal."

"And it's eating our track right now! Stop it!"

"Not too easily done. It spurts acid venom for a hundred metres. It is fierce when aroused, only an atom bomb can stop it..."

"That's it then! We'll put an atom bomb in a metal box and lay it on the track and the dune-buggy will eat it and blow itself up and we will go on happily..."

"A doozy of a plan, sir. Only one small thing wrong with it. We have no atom bomb."

"Killjoy," the Admiral whimpered.

"Congratulations on your promotion, Lieutenant Parrts," Styreen said, opening the fairest eyes in the world and smiling with them. Not an easy thing to do.

"Thank you, Lieutenant Fome. Since we are of equal rank now may I call you . . . Styreen . . .?"

"Just can that stuff!" the Admiral shouted. "How do we get out of this mess you got us into?"

"Simple enough," Styreen said, looking at the giant insect and making an "eck" sound. "We just go around it."

"How?"

"That's your job, Admiral, you're the rail nut around here. How many lectures have I heard on the resourcefulness of the old-time railroaders..."

"Quiet!" The Admiral looked and thought, and smiled. "We'll go around it. Glad I thought of that. We'll tear up some of the track behind us, lay it in front, go ahead, tear it up and re-lay it until we reach the original roadbed again."

"Sounds like a lot of work," Parrts muttered.

"You're damned right. But for you, not me. I'll supervise. Get the troops moving."

The sun set and rose again, and did this a considerable number of times more, while they dragged tracks and sleepers through the desert sands. Muscles bulged where none had flourished before, skins grew red, than tan, except for the lucky few who were black already. The Admiral grew fat from sitting in the cab and eating sandwiches and reading old railroad timetables. But even the largest desert is finally crossed, the biggest dune-buggy circumnavigated. Step by step they crawled forward until they reached the ragged end of the uneaten rails. When they joined up at last, the Admiral wheezed and puffed down from the cab to drive the golden spike. Without a backward look or regret they picked up speed towards the beckoning horizon. They rolled until dusk, revelling in the feeling of speed and progress, and stopped only when darkness fell, for a celebratory banquet. Drink flowed copiously and even the Admiral seemed to be enjoying himself and did not notice when the MP Major passed out. Free of sadistic surveillance for a few brief moments Parrts and Styreen locked fingers under the table and looked meltingly into each other's eyes.

"We are of the same rank now," he moaned. "We can be married, a military ceremony under crossed rayguns."

"How romantic!"

"Then when we get a chance we'll desert and find a lonely planet and live there and night and day we will..."

"Don't say it," she quavered," or we'll be at it right now and the Admiral will kill us both."

"You are so right, Styreen."

"Parrts, darling, is that the only name you have?" "He blushed and lowered his eyes. "I have a first name known to no one."

"Tell me!"

"You'll laugh."

"Never!"

"It's... Percival..."

"Percival Parrts. It's darling. May I call you

Percy?"

"Only if I can call you Styree..."

"This is the most sickening conversation I have heard in my entire life," the MP Major said, waking up, "and I am going to puke."

They were further north now and the nights were getting chill. The desert petered out and the train soon wound its way through hardwood forests with giant trees reaching a hundred metres or more into the air. It was a very scenic ride and they were beginning to enjoy it, which should have been a warning and then they should have knocked wood or bit their tongues, or something, because all too soon the forests gave way to tilled fields.

"Not again," the Admiral moaned, turning blue with fear. "Have we not had enough?"

"Apparently not," Parrts said, "shall I sound the alert?"

They went slower, prepared for anything around each bend, their quavering fingers clutched guns and wary eyes ever on the lookout.

"Those creatures working in the fields look like rats," Parrts said, "only with too many arms."

"Just keep your observations to yourself."

"I think they're cute in a sort of fuzzy way," Styreen said, bringing the Admiral his morning joint. "And look, aren't they bowing towards the train when we pass?"

The Admiral puffed and tried to relax. "Probably the dirtiest gesture they have," he suggested morbidly.

Then, around one last bend, came the inevitable sight. A city wall lay ahead, neatly breached, with their railroad track plowing right through the heart of the metropolis.

"I'm getting too old for this job," the Admiral moaned, "couldn't that rotten RRAGG have missed *one* town?"

"But this one is different, sir," Parrts advised. "They've built a gateway over the tracks, there's a big station there, flags, bands, a reception. A welcoming party!"

"I know enough about the welcoming parties on this planet. Let's get it over with."

Whistle tooting they rattled ahead, their guns ready and disbelieving of everything they saw. Cheering throngs, waving paws and flags, bagpipes screeching, bass drums beating. Ever so slowly they eased into the station, reeking of suspicion, glumly eyeing the splendidly garbed welcoming committee. They could have kept on through the station, the tracks appeared to be unobstructed.

"Just wave and we'll keep moving," the Admiral said.

"Doesn't seem fair," Styreen pouted, "they've gone to so much effort for us, building this lovely station and everything."

"Who gives a damn. Onwards!"

But having just bellowed his rallying command, Soddy had to immediately slam on the brakes to avoid ramming a ramshackle steam loco that had appeared suddenly on the tracks ahead of them. They screeched to a halt alongside the red carpet and everyone in the station cheered. A splendidly-garbed figure stepped forward.

"Welcome, oh mighty trainmen, welcome to Kroo."

"You speak pretty good English for a rat," the Admiral said, suspiciously.

"How charming of you to say so, Admiral. Will you and your staff join us at the reception?"

"How do you know my first name?" he asked, unmoving.

"From our good friends, the noble Gornishthilfen. They report that they got safely away with your aid, so the carnivorous and vile Slimians have been deprived of their big Friday fish feed. They speak very well of you despite the fact you parking-lotted their home world. They also said to tell you they have arranged transportation to another planet so you

ET RECS -- DEPT BIO-CONTACTS -- PROJ REF CO-ORD -- STRAB862

COPYRIGHT U.S.E. DEPT/ INT'SR AFFAIRS BY KIND PERMISSION ET RECS BIO·CONTACTS DIV.
LEFT SP STEREO PAIR REF STRABEM26210·VS(L) OFFICIAL EXPEDITION RECORD
POST RRAGG DISASTER (STRABISMUS) / SODDY DEBACLE HOMO/STRAB PRE·TECH 'RODENT' TYPE INTERFACE (ZERO ZERO ONE SIX ON SCHMIDT SCALE)
SEE ET RECS BIO·CONTACTS CATALOG FOR OTHER BIO TYPES RE THIS INTERFACE

RESTRICTED

won't have to look for them here. But enough talking shop. Please join us at the groaning board. I am King Ratt, this is my wife, Queen Skwirrly, and lots of others."

"Half of you at the banquet, the others at the guns," the Admiral whispered, "I don't trust this rodent ruler."

"But he's got such nice fur," Styreen said.

"And too many paws. That's always a bad sign."

The banquet was not an unqualified success. Too many speeches and the food, old dry cheese and mouldy bread, not of the best. But the wine was good and after a while they were all pretty smashed. It was then that King Ratt gave the closing speech.

"Honoured Earth guests and borderline alcoholics." A ragged cheer went up and there was the sound of breaking glass. "Nice as this banquet was, all good things have to end. And besides, I'm getting kind of tired of hearing jokes like why does it take five rodents to make popcorn, four to shake the stove, and that sort of bushwah. So we better say goodbye and you be on your way. Tell the U.S. of E. how royally you were entertained and what great friends we are so they can keep their parking-lot bombs in the garage. Tell them as well that when they run their trains through here we will charge only the minimal duty on the ore."

"Whuzzah?" the Admiral asked.

"We of Kroo are an honest trading people and as eager to turn an honest buck as the next alien. Since you believe in taxes, duties, surtax, inheritance tax, V.A.T. and such, we have to believe in them too. Also, since we were a railroading people before your machine came along, we appreciate the improvements in track laying it taught us. All we need in Kroo now is some improvements in our trains and we greatly appreciate your aid in this matter and thank you."

"For what?" the Admiral blinked rapidly.

"For changing trains here. We will keep your train and learn from it. Your new train is waiting ahead. We will not stop you now. All change! All change at Kroo!"

"Back to the train!" ordered the Admiral, leaping to his feet. "Stand by to repel boarders."

A number of beady-eyed and nasty rodents suddenly appeared inside the train through freshly chewed holes in the floor, and with rapid ka-rat-y blows disarmed the Earthmen, but otherwise did not injure them.

"How uncivil," King Ratt tsk-tsked. "This is no way to treat a legitimate business deal. I have levied a passage tax equal to the cost of your train and have seized it for non-payment. Out of the goodness of my heart, and memory of the parking-lot bombs, I am giving you our fastest train, the *Mighty Mouse,* for your very own. Supplies are already aboard for your journey and I wish you bon voyage."

The chastised train crew slunk down the platform between the ceremonial spears, now seen to be quite sharp, taking only the clothes they wore.

"This is an outrage!" the Admiral cried.

"This is a receipt," King Ratt said, handing him a very official-looking form, "for your train."

"This is a train?" the Admiral moaned, but his audience had gone; just a few scraps of old bread blew along the platform. A whiskery face leaned out of the control tower ahead and shouted.

"Get that thing moving. The *Furry Flyer* is due in in ten minutes and I don't want no cornfield meets. Out!"

There was already a head of steam up. Parrts tossed another log on the fire and the Admiral pulled the rusty whistle-chain. A thin screeching sounded.

"Not too much on the whistle, Admiral. Pressure just dropped ten pounds."

Steam leaking from every pipe, rusty water dripping, flat wheels clanking, hotbox journals smoking, the *Mighty Mouse* crawled out of the station and headed north.

Locomotive of the type presented to Admiral Soddy
by the 'Rodent Ruler' during the Strabisman Debacle

CHAPTER 10.

SEALE

ED WITH A KISS

"IT'S GETTING COLDER," Styreen shivered.

"Belt up and throw another log on the fire," the Admiral suggested sadistically. "If you're going to ride in the nice warm engine you're going to work for the privilege. How's that leaking joint coming, Parrts?"

"Looks OK now, sir. I made a paste out of the hard cheese and stale bread and the steam cooked it like a rock."

"All that rotten food is good for. They could have left us *one* little case of lobsters. I feel terrible.

"Yes, sir, you look terrible too. Not that any of us are any better, sir," Parrts rushed to add as a look of instant death glittered in Admiral Soddy's eyes. "No food, work all the time, getting colder, it's hell, I tell you, hell!"

"So don't re-enlist," the Admiral yawned, with complete lack of sympathy. "Wood's running out. I'll stop at that next grove of trees. Get the axemen cracking."

There were groans of despair as they clanked to a stop and the filthy, ragged, unshaven staff officers fell to the frozen ground and picked up their axes. Wood burning engines take a lot of wood they had found out.

"Water," Parrts said, pulling the dip stick out of the tank and scowling at it. "Four men to the snow bank there. Plenty of ice and snow."

The wind whistled through the bleak landscape and it began to snow again. Tank filled, tender loaded, they crawled aboard – and stopped, frozen with fear.

"What w-was that?" Styreen trembled.

"A howl, more vicious and evil, more soul-destroying and horrible than anything I have heard before," suggested Parrts.

"What sort of creature could make a sound like that," shivered Styreen, blowing on her chapped hands.

This, being on Strabismus after all, where things always got worse before they got worse, they were not long in finding out. Out of the falling snow plunged giant grey shapes, howling as they came, jaws slavering, teeth gnashing, claws tearing at the ground, red eyes gleaming. You know.

Three hands pulled the throttle wide at the same time. "I drive this thing!" the Admiral grated, and they removed their hands from his. But the idea was right.

Ever so slowly they clanked forwards and the war-wolves were upon them. The travellers kicked at the gnashing jaws that bit big chunks out of the side of the train and beat at the wolves with shovels, which they snapped at and ate. Only speed saved them, or rather the rattling, lurching progress that passed for speed in the *Mighty Mouse.* Very slowly they pulled ahead of the howling grey forms. But they knew that they were still on their trail.

"What happens when we stop for fuel?" Parrts said brightly.

"Shut your stupid mouth," Styreen miffed.

It took him five minutes on his knees, slobbering apologies, before she would even speak to him again. Meanwhile, the Admiral was peering ahead into the snow-filled sky and thinking. The chill in his synapses made thought a slow and painful process these days. "You know, Parrts is right" he finally said. "So before we have to stop again we'll throw someone off the train. Starting with the lowest ranks, of course."

"That's heartless and cruel," Styreen gasped.

"Should I start with the lieutenants maybe?" the Admiral leered.

"Your plan does have merits," she admitted. "But why don't we use the bread and cheese first?"

"Good idea. Maybe they can eat it, I know we can't. And that way we save the troops for hard work before we have to throw them overboard."

And the plan worked and many a war-wolf had an aching jaw and splintered teeth that day. Great fangs that could crush bone and rock fractured when attacking the rodent rations. Curses were howled and the pursuit taken up again and the train, having stopped to refuel, pulled out just before their arrival.

"This can't go on for too long" Parrts said. "We'll run out of supplies or hit a snow drift or something."

"Oh, you're really full of wit and wisdom today. Keep feeding the fire."

As darkness began to fall their spirits fell with it.

The food was gone, yet still the tireless, savage forms loped in pursuit. More of them, too. Their store of wood was almost gone and they were crossing a treeless steppe.

"Start breaking up the seats and throw them in."

Smoke puffed out blackly again, but no blacker than their spirits. Night was falling. And ahead in the growing darkness was something even darker.

"The tunnel mouth!" the Admiral shouted.

"We're saved!"

"No we're not," Parrts cassandra'd, "they'll follow us into the tunnel and there will be no wood or water there and they will catch up...*wait!*" He shouted this last because the Admiral had him by the shoulders, Styreen by the legs, both about to throw him off the train. Things were bad enough without his making them sound worse. "Wait! I have a plan! The tunnel will be our salvation."

Doubtfully, they eased him back and he clutched the pipes feebly. "Some joke, ha-ha. Listen, we set fire to the last car, get it burning merrily when we come to the tunnel, uncouple it and leave it in the entrance. Then we make our getaway."

"A plan born of desperation" the Admiral admitted. "But the only chance we got. Get cracking."

The last car was emptied and hurriedly set on fire. The dry wood blazed up and Parrts fled back to the next car, leaning far out to grab the pin in the archaic lincoln-pin coupling.

"We're in the tunnel – let go!" Styreen shouted, and he pulled.

The train kept going but the car dropped behind, filling the tunnel with flame and the sound of the frustrated howls of the war-wolves.

"Safe at last." Styreen was elated.

"As soon as the fire burns out they'll be past it . . . AIEEE!" Parrts screamed this last because Styreen, fed up at last, had booted him off the train. He ran after the last car, calling feebly and stumbling in the darkness, until love overcame disgust and she slowed the train so he could catch up. After this there was very little negativity on his part, you betcha!

It was a race now against time, if clattering along at twenty kilometres an hour can be called a race, to see if they reached the end before they ran out of combustibles. The train grew shorter and shorter as they fed it into the furnace and left the odd burning coach to stop the panting, yet still pursuing war-wolves. Then two coaches were left, finally one, and still there was no end in sight. After gutting the last car and setting it alight as a final blockade, the exhausted survivors clung to the engine of *Mighty Mouse* and huddled in the rapidly emptying tender. There was still some wood left when the Admiral suddenly jammed on the brakes. Feeble fists pummelled his shoulders and even feebler voices urged him to go on.

"I can't" he insisted. "The track ends here."

They tumbled down to the cold rock floor and saw that, indeed the track did end abruptly. In the smoking beam of the headlight they read the words graven in the stone of the wall.

SORRY, RAN OUT OF TRACK.
BUT YOU HAVE ONLY 5 KMS.
TO GO AND THE WALK WILL
DO YOU GOOD. GIVE MY
REGARDS TO MY DEAR FRIEND,
ADMIRAL SODDY.
RRAGG

"Your dear friend is going to send you screaming to the junkyard when he gets back," the Admiral gnashed. "Let's move it because I do think I hear a familiar howling behind us."

This moved them all out rather briskly, except for Parrts.

"Go on, my dearest," he said, "and I will catch you up in a while."

"What are you planning to do?" Styreen screamed.

"Go with the others and I'll be right along."

Simple survival warred in her heart with eternal love and a moment later she was trotting after the others. They gasped and stumbled through the darkness – but halted suddenly when a great explosion echoed behind them. Then stood, paralysed, as running feet and panting breath approached.

"Be quick, wolf," Styreen said, "for this is the end."

"It's me" Parrts panted. "The wolves are dead. I rigged a chain to the safety valve and put all the wood into the boiler. The valve popped and I waited until the wolves were at the engine, then closed the valve and ran. The boiler blew."

"My genius," Styreen sighed.

"My feet hurt," the Admiral grumbled. "Let's get this trip over with."

It was an exhausted, stumbling, yet happy mob of ragged survivors who staggered out of the tunnel mouth into the polar blizzard. The space tug was there and it was a close run thing if they would freeze to death or make it. They made it, of course, and collapsed into the airlock. But food and drink restored them and the Admiral reassumed command.

"Pilot!"

"Sir!"

"Is the prefab Mine Superintendent's building here?"

"Aye, aye, sir. It has been prefabbed and stocked with food and is standing out there in the eternal snows in spartan simplicity waiting for the poor bugger who will man it."

"No problem there. Lieutenant Parrts step forward." Thick fingers groped greedily and there was a ripping sound and Parrts's bars rattled to the deck. "Private Parrts, I have an assignment for you. We are leaving now and you will remain here, alone forever, in charge of the robot mining equipment."

"You can't do that!"

"I've done it!"

"You promised to shoot me, a far better fate."

"So I break my promise. This way I get a bit of sadism thrown in for nothing. Because *I* have your fiancée Styreen Fome." Chortling wickedly he clutched her trembling form to his gross one and it took five strong troopers to seize and hold Parrts and boot him out into the snow, to drag him to the prefab and push him inside. They could hear his angry shouts even after they had closed the airlock and only the blast of the rockets on take-off drowned him out.

For Parrts it was the end, even more than the end because soon after the space tug had left he received a call from the radio operator aboard it.

"I'm sorry to be the bearer of ill tidings, Superintendent, but we have had a suicide aboard the ship and the suicide left a note for you in the airlock. The outer door was open."

"No ill tidings," Parrts gloated. "I hope it was painful for the Admiral when he went. Read me what he said."

"Wasn't no Admiral. Was a Lieutenant name of Fome." Parrts's scream echoed horribly but the operator kept on speaking, getting the unhappy duty over with so he could get back to his bottle, bunk, and lifesized dildo. 'Darling' that's what the note says, I didn't say that cause I'm square. 'Darling. This is the end. I cannot face the thought of eternity without your embraces and those of the swine Admiral instead. My love will burn forever. S.W.A.K. Your Styree.' Message ends. Over and out."

It was the end for Parrts too. Oh, he would go on, living for her memory, doing his job, but a husk of a man with his soul burned away. A drinking man who reached for the bottle and drained half of it and was scarcely aware.

There he was, the last man in the world, alone in the room.

There was a knock at the door.

"War-wolves," he muttered blearily, "Or Slimians, lobsters, rats, something nasty. I'll open the door and kill it."

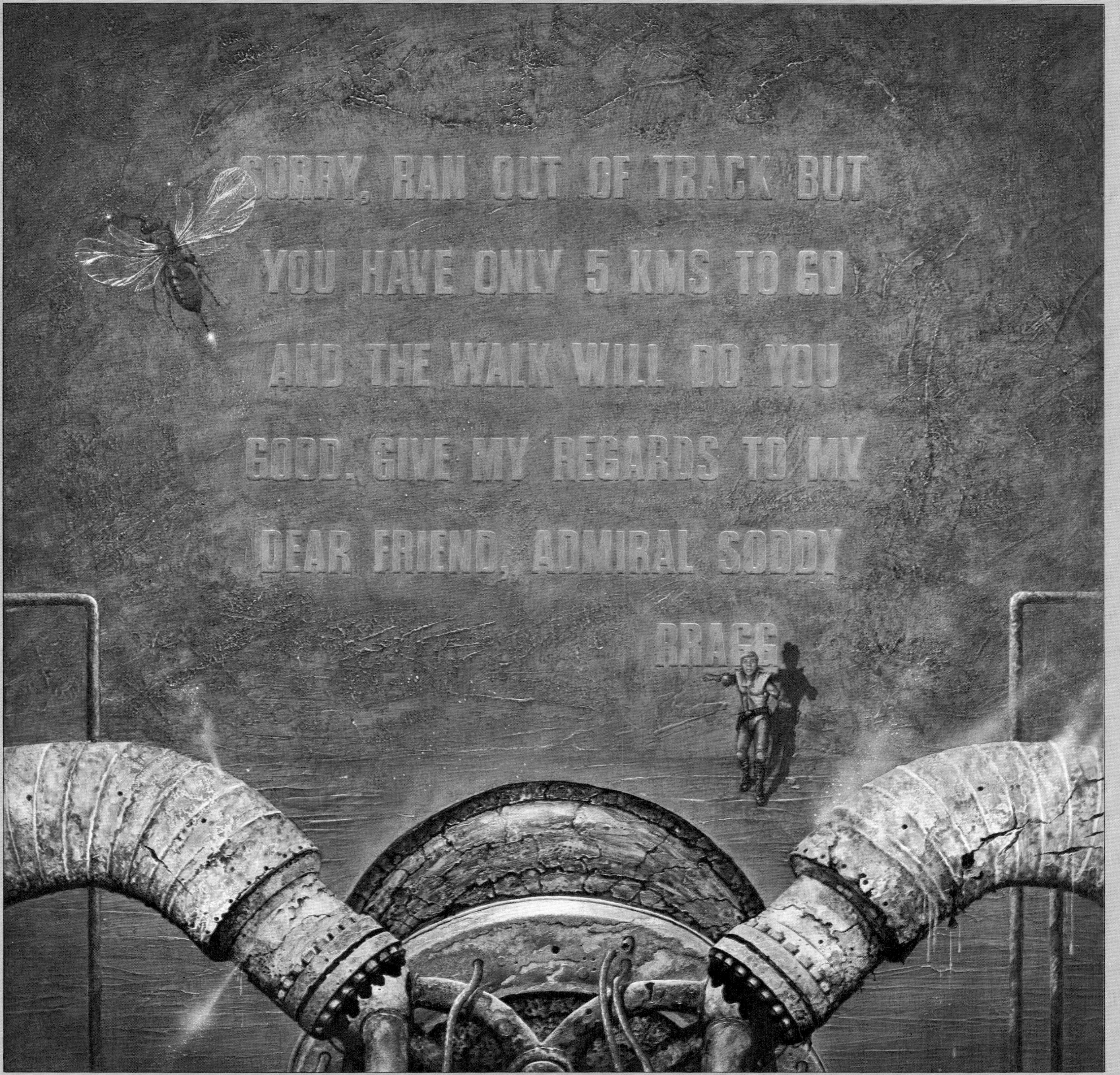

SORRY, RAN OUT OF TRACK BUT
YOU HAVE ONLY 5 KMS TO GO
AND THE WALK WILL DO YOU
GOOD. GIVE MY REGARDS TO MY
DEAR FRIEND, ADMIRAL SODDY

BRAGG

He opened the door and the luscious form of Styreen fell into his arms.

"Glug!" he said.

"I know how you feel," she whispered. "But life was empty without you. I stole a spacesuit with a retropak, wrote a suicide note, then jumped. Landed just outside. I just took time to get out of that ugly suit, comb my hair and put on lipstick before I knocked, because I knew you would be worried..."

He kicked the door shut and...

And we will draw the curtain ever so quietly on these two. Is that a tear I see in your eye? Don't be ashamed for there is a tear in mine too. In these days of galactic war, usurious income tax, yobbo football riots, watered beer and cirrhosis, isn't it nice to know that somewhere, at the end of the universe, at the coldest pole of a distant planet, two people are divinely happy? Let us dream their dream with them. Let us hope that for every young lad there will be a Styreen Fome, for every lass Private Parrts.

JIM BURNS

Jim Burns was born on the 10th April 1948 in Cardiff, South Wales. In 1966 he left school to take up a career as a trainee pilot in the R.A.F. his life long ambition, but left having soloed on 'Chipmunks' and 'Jet Provosts' after eighteen months. To return to flying in a private capacity is still a great ambition.

In 1968 he began his art training at Newport School of Art in London England and spent four years there, ending with a Graphic Design Course. His diploma show was seen by John Spencer of the Young Artists agency and he was taken on by them immediately. Since then he has been working without a break, mostly in the Science Fiction area, doing jacket work and paperback book covers. PLANET STORY is his first complete work.

HARRY HARRISON

Born in the United States far too long ago, this author has been referred to as being singularly peripatetic – although he can't spell the word – and has travelled and resided in a number of countries including Denmark, Italy, Bromley, France, Spain, Mexico and the Camden Town Road. Today he resides in Ireland, on the shore within sight of Joyce's Martello Tower and not a stone's throw from a pub where he keeps an account. He is the author of twenty-five novels, five short story collections and has edited so many anthologies that he stopped counting. Harrison has stated in public that PLANET STORY is the crowning achievement of his career and he will enter a monastery as soon as it is published. However he said it in the pub, mentioned above, so the veracity is open to doubt.